"No—it is forbidden!"

Arvicola's whisper was frantic. In the fading glow, Barber could see his reflection in a big mirror; and beneath that mirror on a little shelf lay Titania's crook-handled wand.

He snatched for the wand. As his hand touched it, he noticed lettering deeply engrailed on the glass:

> *On the pathway you trace*
> *The face that you face*
> *Is the median place.*

"Come—oh, quick!" Arvicola gripped his wrist urgently. He pulled loose and reached for the mirror with the tip of the wand.

A violent electric shock ran up his arm and all through him. Before he could analyze it, he was aware of a new, deep darkness; a shapeless *something* that almost filled the chamber, with two expressionless eyes that reflected . . .

Land of Unreason

L. Sprague de Camp
and
Fletcher Pratt

A DELL BOOK

Published by
DELL PUBLISHING CO., INC.
1 Dag Hammarskjold Plaza
New York, N.Y. 10017

A shorter version of this novel appeared in the
October 1941 issue of *Unknown Worlds.*

Dell ® TM 681510, Dell Publishing Co., Inc.

ISBN: 0-440-14736-0

Reprinted by arrangement with L. Sprague de Camp
Printed in the United States of America
First Dell printing—March 1979

To
John D. Clark,
Another hard-boiled rationalist, and
for all we know, Another
Fred Barber

Land of Unreason

CHAPTER I

As the torn clouds trailed out in wisps and streaks, the moon seemed to rock among them with a boatlike motion, rising over the Pennine moors. Small wonder, thought Fred Barber, that peoples as far apart as Assyria and Hawaii made it the celestial ship of their mythology. One needed only a certain ignorance of the true character of natural phenomena, a certain practical familiarity with the effect of wave motion on a floating craft—provided, of course, that the common craft of the country, the thing one instinctively thought of when someone said "ship," were round, with high ends . . .

Beside him Mr. Gurton grunted, spat into a warm night redolent of broom and dog rose, and reached across to knock his pipe against the doorpost. The few last live sparks in the heel traced an intricate pattern down the dark.

"Time were," remarked Mr. Gurton, "when I'd have said that looked beautiful. Nah all a man can think of is t'damned Jerries on our necks befoor moornin'."

As though to furnish a comment on the relative unimportance of Jerries in a world that held higher things a voice called from within: "Sooper's ready."

Barber crushed out his cigarette and took two steps toward the door. As he turned, the tail of his eye caught in the moonlit landscape a flicker of something that did not belong. He froze, at gaze. It was there, all right—a jagged row of crimson flashes climbing up the sky from some point below the horizon. Barber caught his breath.

"Leed's is catchin' it," said Mr. Gurton's low-pitched, evenly stressed voice. They stood watching for a moment till the dull *boom, boom, beroom* drifted to them along the avenue of sound made by the valley of the Aire. Then Gurton, with a sudden jerking movement, as though the noise had released him from a spell, flung the door open.

It snapped to behind them, and with an extra tug to ensure its tightness Gurton led the way down a passage illuminated only by an overflow of light from the living room. He jerked his thumb at a curtained door as they passed it. "Bloody fine world to bring a nipper oop in," said he.

Mrs. Gurton accosted them at the entrance to the living room, a thin-faced woman with hair pulled tight back and nervous hands. "Ssh, Jock," she said, "don't you know it's St. John's Eve? They say 'twill bring t'child bad loock all his life long to talk so abaht him tonight." She managed a smile in Barber's direction, but there was a hint of earnestness in the voice and the movement with which she caught her apron.

Gurton smiled slowly. "Nah, lass," he said, with the patience of a man going over the gambits of a long-familiar argument, "that's nowt boot superstition. What would vicar say?" He sighed. "Maybe t'flashes we saw were nowt boot fairy-fires."

Boom, Boomity. Boom.

They began to eat. Barber, surveying the soggy meal before him, reflected that he was becoming a culinary chauvinist. Spanish cooking burned his insides. It was probably invented to enable Spanish cooks to conceal the fact that they were serving horse meat instead of the beef they were given money to buy. "Si, señor," said Ramón, the cook at the Seville consulate, when Barber explained to him the mysteries of two-inch-

thick broiled steak, the night the Congressman from
Texas came for dinner. "Si, señor," and it had indubitably been horse meat and the Congressman's
wife was sick. With a certain grim amusement Barber
recalled his own horrified realization that the man was
on the Foreign Relations Committee, and the black
scowl with which the Congressman regarded that
horse-meat steak meant that Fred Barber's career in
diplomacy was probably over. It had seemed very important at the time, that horrible dinner, much more
important than the fact that they were using ersatz
coffee in Germany and selling the butter to buy
guns. . . .

Boom. Boomm!

"That were Bradford," remarked Mr. Gurton.

Oh, hell, why couldn't the war let him alone? Why
couldn't he let the war alone? They would be at it
again, half the night. Must everything he did, everything he ate or touched or thought, remind him of it,
keep him lying sleepless and twisting? There was the
bottle of Scotch, of course, kept side for an emergency,
which might be tonight. The thought was more dis-
quieting than comforting. That was the insomnia cure
he had been trying to get away from. That was the
reason why he was here.

He wished he had gone on to Scotland, as he had
planned, instead of letting young Leach talk him into
finishing his convalescence in a Yorkshire cottage. "I
know just the place for you." Damn young Leach for
a plausible, well-intentioned ass! It was the plausible,
well-intentioned people that made the real trouble in
the world, not the malicious ones. If Chamberlain had
not been . . .

Mr. Gurton set his knife against his plate with a
small clink and looked at the clock. It read 10:45. He
said: "Let's have t'savory, lass." As Mrs. Gurton was
taking away the remnants of his supper, he remarked
apologetically to Barber: "You see, t'foor-to-midneet

chap on ma drill press is a lazy booger; 'as a rotten
'abit o' lettin' it roon dry, and I want to get theer i'
time to see her well oiled oop."

BOOM!

The dishes rattled slightly. The savory was a slice of
toast upon which reposed a small and very dead sardine. Mrs. Gurton said: "I kept your toast 'ot special,
Mr. Barber."

"Thanks ever so much," said Barber. It was lukewarm. Mr. Gurton picked up his sardine with a long,
knobby, oil-blackened hand. It vanished and his own
decently frigid toast with it.

Lukewarm, thought Barber, with his mind divided
into two parts. One part ran desperately around a
great black hole that was the war and all the things
that came up out of it and went down into it. Lukewarm, said the other part, and he tried to distract
himself with the question of why Luke should be less
warm than the other evangelists. Why not Matthew-
warm, Mark-warm, John-warm? Why the evangelists
for that matter? Why not Adolf-warm, which would
be hell-hot? . . .

Boomboom.

Mr. Gurton rose and put on a cloth cap, with a
creased and sagging peak that shadowed all of a cadav-
erous face except his long chin. He said: "You'll not
worry, Mr. Barber. Unless they come this way to bomb
Keighley, all's well 'ere. Good neet." His brisk tread
hardly showed the limp as he went to get his bicycle
and pedal off to work.

Mrs. Gurton looked after him calmly. The door
banged, and all at once a stream of conversation burst
from her lips, as though the small stimulus of the
sound had released a spring that held her tongue
prisoner. The war, the war, Barber's mind kept saying to him from the background, his ears only partly
registering this monotonous flow of sound.

". . . ma aunt's yoong man. I remember 'e were 'urt

i' t' gurt war, joost t'way Jock 'ere, only it were a shell and noot a aeroplane bomb that fell i' t'trench joost when they were 'avin' breekfast and 'e were eatin' ploom-and-apple, and always after that whenever 'e 'eered a sharp sound like a mautercar backfirin' it made him retch, and 'e did say it were all because he saw a black cat . . ."

Taptap.

Bombs that tapped? No, door. Mrs. Gurton was opening. The lamplight fell dimly on a small boy with the plucked look English small boys have and a bicycle, and an anxious, excited face. He should be calmed with light conversation. "Calm them with light conversation before undertaking the diplomatic approach," Barber's old chief in the State Department had told him before letting him go out on his first mission, vice-consul at Seville. The boy was talking in a high voice:

"Please, moom, a gurt bomb 'it near t' Winstanley's 'oose, and Mrs. Winstanley's 'urt soomat nasty and Dr. Thawley says please would you coom . . ."

"Wait a bit," said Mrs. Gurton. Barber saw the eyes regard him sharply over her shoulder as she picked up her shawl.

He stood up a little too quickly; his head began to throb. He said: "Can't I—"

"Nah, Mr. Barber, remember what t'doctor telled you; s'ouldn't strain yoursen. You go off to bed like a good lad." She was out the door before he had a chance to argue—the back door, on some errand, then in again, through the house and out the front door into the warm light, where things went boom-boom.

Barber slumped back into the uncomfortable chair, his legs spreading to find an easier angle. His head ached. It was not that one feared death after having the possibility so long as a familiar companion. It was this damned waiting for it or anything else decisive to happen. It would be almost a relief. "Fate worse than death"—he had laughed with the rest of the audience at the line when it had been used in a comedy revival of an old-fashioned melodrama. Well, there were fates worse than death. One of them was living on and waiting to drop dead after being clipped on the head by a bomb splinter or piece of shrapnel (he had never learned which) as you ran out of the Embassy into the night when the German raiders came. British or German? German or British? Somebody had thrown into that night a missile that struck a neutral American in a quarrel that was none of his own. Diplomatic immunity did not, he reflected, exist in the material world. It was a purely spiritual quality, and he was feeling sorry for himself, which . . .

Boom. Boom.

Oh, for heaven's sake! Why couldn't they let up? Why couldn't anybody let up? If he had been more sure of Kaja, of where she might be spending that night when the bombers came, he wouldn't have run out of the Embassy. If he could be more sure of Kaja now, he wouldn't be miserable. He allowed his mind to dwell on Kaja, pleasant thought, her red hair and long silky legs, and the fact that although she had a straight nose and Hungarian name and claimed to be from Budapest, she was unquestionably Jewish.

Kaja, pleasant thought, always looking light enough to fly. The fragment of a song occurred to him—"I wonder who's kissing her now"—and he smiled wryly. Anybody who could buy her enough Scotch. Kaja preferred Scotch to champagne. It was a good drink, Scotch. Useful when a man couldn't sleep.

He got up, more slowly this time, and dug out his bottle of Scotch, pouring himself a hefty dram. He swashed it around in the glass, staring at the pale-orange liquid. Useful stuff, but only up to a limit. What was his limit? The limit of a diplomatic career which had already reached its limit when he fed horse meat to the Congressman. Oh, damn! Oh, hell! It might have been all right but for this war, might have been forgotten if foreign affairs had not become so tense that every member of the service was forced, so to speak, to operate in a show window, with his name constantly under Congressional scrutiny. And Kaja . . . ? He lifted the glass.

Beroom.

And set it down again. With a trick of automatic memory his mind had jerked back to the picture of Mrs. Gurton going out the back door. She had had something in her hand, a bowl, a bowl of . . . milk. Milk? The Gurtons didn't keep a cat. Why milk to the back door?

Fred Barber remembered that Mrs. Gurton had said this was St. John's Eve, the twenty-third of June, the day before Midsummer Day. Oh, yes, something in *The Golden Bough.* You leave milk out for the Little People that night, especially if there is a baby in the house, for unless the Little People receive their tribute they are likely to steal the child and leave a change-ling. Interesting survival; who would have believed that a woman whose husband ran a drill press in a munitions factory and who herself went to nurse a neighbor through a bomb wound, would leave milk at the door for fairies? Almost worth writing a sardonic little note about, to be sent to the *New Yorker* which would return him a check no doubt, to be spent on Scotch for Kaja.

Milk.

Fred Barber liked milk, a fact which he concealed with the most painful care from the gay, interesting, mocking crowd in London. He had been brought up on a drink of milk before bedtime. It made him sleep. But the war and milk rationing had made him go without, like many others to whom milk was more of a hobby than a necessity. Mrs. Gurton could have it for the baby of course. But if she were going to give it to the fairies, why, Fred Barber argued to himself

with a grin, he was as good a fairy as any who would
be abroad that night. The mission of fairies was to
bring gifts and he was bringing the Gurtons a pound
sterling a week.

Milk. The mere idea of drinking it instead of the
Scotch gave him a sense of virtue and power. What
was it Nietzsche had said: "Every conquest is the result of courage, of hardness towards one's self"? Well,
he would conquer, in spite of the crack on the head.
His mind flashed back to the determination with
which he had set out on his career. If he could recover
some of that, the old pep, a little crack on the head
wouldn't matter. He could demonstrate a capacity for
hardness to himself, recall the sense of destiny that had
filled him once. To hell with the Scotch, and Kaja
too. He strode to the door, his mind so intent on the
peculiar nobleness of using milk instead of Scotch as
a sleeping powder that he carried the glass with him.

The moonlight showed the bowl, sure enough, a
pale circle beside one of the flowerpots that lined the
back of the cottage. Barber stuck his finger in the
bowl and tasted. It was milk—trust Mrs. Gurton. He
set down the glass, and as the bombs in the distance
continued their infernal beat, lifted the bowl in both
hands, drinking slowly and with relish.

Over the edge of the vessel he could see the red
glow that marked something burning in Bradford,
with searchlight beams flickering cobwebby above.
And what would the fairies of St. John's Eve do now,
poor things, with no milk, and bombs falling on their
heads? Fred Barber set the bowl down, and then
grinned like a small boy in the dark as inspiration
came to him. They could drink Scotch!

He poured the slug of Scotch into the bowl, watching the last dregs of the milk weave through it, and
chuckled at the thought of Mrs. Gurton's expression
when she found the milk of which she had robbed
the baby so mysteriously transmuted. The delicious

sense of languor in every limb that presaged instant slumber was still wanting, as it had been ever since his injury, but he knew now it would come, he was at peace.

The trouble with these English feather beds, though, was not merely that they were too warm for the twenty-third of June, but also that you went right on down through the softness till you hit a bump. There was one under his hip and he shifted position to avoid it. Wonderful people, these English— His carefully cultivated cynicism broke down when he contemplated them. Fairies and machine shops and courage under bombings—like something out of a poem by Walter de la Mare. Or Masefield. Yes, especially Masefield.

His mind swung lazily into contemplation of the essential rightness of choosing Masefield as the poet laureate of this people, for whom he wished he could do something—then drifted into a hazy picture of Masefield characters, all mingled with fairies, Kaja and the Gurtons. He came to with a start, realizing that he had almost been asleep. Without regrets, he drifted into a blankness of thoughts half formed . . .

Tik.

The door hinge, faintly, as though someone had moved the door through a few minutes of arc. Then again—tik—tik—tik, tik tik, tiktiktik.

Barber, fully awake now, looked toward the door. It was open, and something coming through it. He couldn't be sure in the gloom, but it looked like a face, an incredible face that might have come from a comic strip. The loose lips were drawn back in a grin so extended that the corners of the mouth were out of sight. For all Barber could tell the grin went all the way round and met at the back, like Humpty Dumpty's. The ears were pendulous; over the grin was a head utterly hairless but bearing a pair of knobbed antennae.

Oh, well, *that,* said Fred Barber to himself, and

with that strange double vision, outside and inside of one's personality, that comes at the edge of sleep, felt certain he was dreaming and slipped down into the blank again.

CHAPTER II

He was lying on his side, one arm curled under his head and blue moonlight all around him. Bright moonlight: one could read newsprint in such an illumination, he reflected in the first half second of returning consciousness, and then write to Ripley about it. Somewhere in the "Believe It or Not" collections was the statement that the feat was impossible. If . . .

He became aware that the fingers of the hand underneath were touching grass and heaved himself to a sitting posture, now bolt wide-awake. From beyond his own feet the face of the dream was grinning under knobbed antennae, which pricked eagerly toward him like the horns of a snail. Behind, Barber was conscious of other crowding figures as he tried to concentrate on what Knob-horns was saying.

". . . mickle bit o' work, moom." Knob-horns spread arms and let the hands dangle from a pair of loose wrists, slightly swaying like a tight-rope walker. " 'E were that 'eavy. *'ic.*"

There was a little ripple of suppressed amusement behind Barber, with a clear contralto voice rising out of it:

"Wittold! Is't so you were taught to address the Queen's Majesty? What said you?"

The mobile features regrouped themselves from a grin into an expression of comic and formidable sullenness.

"I said 'e were 'eavy."

"Aye. One needs not your ass's ears to have caught so much. But after that?"

Barber swiveled. The contralto belonged to a beauty, built on the ample lines of a show-girl chorus he had once seen, justifiably advertised as the "Ten Titanic Swede-hearts." He caught a glimpse of patrician nose, masterful chin, dark hair on which rode a diadem with a glowing crescent in front.

The being with the antennae replied: "I said nowt after that. '*ic*."

Barber experienced the odd sensation of being informed by some sixth sense that the individual was not quite sure of his own veracity. The tall lady had no such doubts:

"Ah, 'tis time for a shaping, indeed," she cried, "when my husband makes messengers of louts that lie barefaced! What is't, I asked, some new form of address in mock compliment from my gentle lord? You said *Ic!*"

Antennae shifted his feet, opened his mouth and abruptly fell down. The others clustered around him, twittering, babbling and pushing, a singular crowd.

Some were as tall as Barber, and some small, down to a foot in height, and their appearance was as various as their size. Many, especially of the smaller ones, had wings growing out of their backs; some were squat and broad, as though a gigantic hand had pushed them groundward while they were in a semi-fluid state. An individual with a beard and wall eyes that gave him an expression of perpetual surprise was dressed like a Palmer Cox brownie; others wore elaborate clothes that might have been thought up by King Richard II, and some had no more clothes than a billiard ball.

Pink elephants, thought Barber, or am I going nuts? One half of his mind was rather surprised to find the other considering the question with complete detachment.

"What ails yon wight?" demanded the regal lady, who had not condescended to join the crowd.

The brownie looked around. "A sleeps; plain insensible like a stockfish, and snoring." There was a chatter of other voices: "An enchantment, for sure— Send for Dos Erigu . . . The leprechauns again, they followed the king . . . Nay, that's no prank, 'tis sheer black kobbold malice . . ."

"Peace!" The contralto cut sharply across the other voices, and she extended her arm. Barber saw that she held a slender rod about a foot long, with a point of light at its tip. "If there's sorcery here we'll soon have it unsorcelled. Azam-mancestu-monejalma—stol!" The point of light leaped from the tip of the rod, and moved through the air with a sinuous, flowing motion. It lit on the forehead of the antennaed one, where it spread across his features till they seemed to glow from within. He grunted and turned over, a fatuous smile spreading across his face, but did not wake. The tall lady let arm and rod fall.

"Pah!" said she. "Like a stockfish, you put it? Say a stock rather; here's no enchantment but a booby with barely wit enough to live. Oh, I'm well served." She gazed down at Barber, with an expression of scorn on her delicately cut features. "And here he's brought this great oafish ill-favored creature, beyond doubt the least attractive changeling of the current reign."

Barber was being scrutinized. "Think you His Radiance will acccept the thing?" inquired one doubtfully.

The tall lady sighed. "We can but try. Mayhap 'twill find him in his mad humor and so suit. See to the object; we return within an hour." She swept off into a little grove of trees through which the pillars of some structure gleamed whitely.

The one who had spoken last, a winged female about four feet high, bent over Barber, examining his pajamas. "He has arrived without his clout," she said. "Have we one?"

A square of whitish cloth was passed from hand to hand. The four-footer folded it diagonally and tried to roll Barber over.

"Hey!" he protested. "What's the idea?"

"The changeling speaks," said one of them, in an astonished tone. "Faith, and well," replied another, admiringly. "What precocity! His Radiance will, after all, be pleased." And half a dozen of them went off into peals of gay, tinkling laughter. Barber could see neither rhyme nor reason to it, but he was not granted the opportunity, as at the same moment he was seized by a dozen pairs of busy hands. They were trying to diaper him; the idea was so comic that he could not stop laughing enough to resist. But neither could these queer little people control his movements well enough to get the diaper on, and the struggle ended with three or four of them collapsing on top of him in a tangle of arms and legs.

The four-footer said gravely: "Marry, 'tis no small problem with so lusty a babe. A very Wayland or Brian of Born when a gets growth, I'll warrant. Yet stay, friends; this is a wise, intelligent brat that talks like a lawyer, that is, never but to his own profit. He merely protests that we put the clout on over his breeches when it should go under. Come, once more!"

She gave a little leap, flapping her wings in excitement, and was bounced a dozen yards into the air by the effort. Barber gaped, following her with his eyes, and felt his pajamas seized by hands eager to tear them off him. He clutched, turned, swung his arms in good, angry embarrassment, then broke loose—even the largest of them did not seem very strong—and backed a few steps against one of the trees, a torn pajama-leg dangling about his feet. Half a dozen of those with wings were in the air. He could hear the whisper of their flight behind the tree, and a chilly hand, small like a child's, plucked from behind at the neck of his too-light upper garment.

"Listen!" he cried. "Unless this is one of those nightmares where you go down Fifth Avenue without your clothes, my name's Fred Barber, and I'll keep my pants, please. You can trust me not to disgrace them. Now, will somebody tell me what this is all about, and why you want to put that thing on me?"

He pointed to the enormous diaper, which had slipped from the hand of its holder and lay spread and tousled on the grass. There was a momentary silence, through which one or two of the aerial creatures planed lightly to the ground, spilling the air from their wings like pigeons. Through it the observant part of Barber's mind shouted to him that in dreams one does not speak but communicate, thought to thought; nor do the fantasies born of head injury follow from step to step. This must, then—

The brownie with the wall eyes had stepped forward, pulled off a striped stocking-cap and was bowing to the ground. "Worshipful babe," he said, in a high, squeaky voice, "you do speak in terms rank reasonable; which, since all reason is folly and I am the court's chief fool, to wit, its philosopher, I give myself to answer in the same terms. As to your first premise, that you dream, why, that's in nature a thing unknowable; for if it were true, the dream itself would furnish the only evidence by which it could be judged. You will agree, worshipful babe, that it's not good law, nor sense either, that one should be at once judge, jury, prosecutor and condemned in his own case. Therefore—"

He was thrust aside in mid-speech by the little winged creature, who cried: "Oh, la! Never speak reasonably to a philosopher, Master Barber; it leads to much words and little wit. What this learned dunce would say in an hour or two is that you find yourself at the court of King Oberon—"

"As mortals have before," chorused half a dozen of them, singing the words like a refrain.

"—About to be made a present of to His Radiance—"

"Do you mean this is really Fairyland?" Barber's voice was incredulous. There was a great burst of laughter from the queer little people all round him, some holding their sides, some slapping knees, others rolling on the ground with mirth till they bumped into each other. Inconsequentially, they turned the movement into a series of acrobatic somersaults and games of leapfrog, laughing all the while.

"Where thought you else?" demanded the winged lady.

"I didn't. But look here—I'm not sure that I want to be a present to King Oberon, like a—like a—" His mind fumbled for the impressive simile, all the time busy with the thought that, in spite of its sequence and vividness, this must be some special kind of hallucination. "—Like an object," he finished lamely. Over behind his interlocutor the playful hobgoblins were slowing down like a weary phonograph record. She held up two little hands with jewels flashing on the fingers.

"Oh, la, Sir Babe, you to question the desire of a crowned king? Why, put it if you must that it's a thing natural, like being born or having two legs. You have no election in the matter. Nay, more—no mortal ever but gained by doing the King's will of Fairyland."

Once more Barber experienced the operation of that curious sixth sense. There was something definitely untrue about that last statement. But this was his game; this was the kind of verbal fencing he had been trained in, and if this whole crazy business were an illusion, so much the better, he could argue himself out of it.

"No doubt," he said evenly, "I shall benefit. But why pick on me? Certainly there must be dozens of people willing to be—pet poodles for King Oberon. You say it's a natural thing. Well, after all, nature has laws, and I'd like to know under what one I was kidnaped. And I'm not a babe."

Once more there was the paroxysm of laughter from the crowd, and the ensuing antics. The winged lady looked bewildered and seemed about to burst into tears, but the brownie philosopher struggled from the grip of a dwarf who had been holding a hand over his mouth, and stepped forward, bowing.

"Nay, Lady Violanta," he said. "By y'r leave, I'll speak, for I perceive by my arts that this is a most sapient babe, so well versed in precepts logical that he'll crush your feather spirit like a bull a butterfly. Let me but have him; I'll play matador to his manners." He bowed, addressing himself to Barber.

"Masterful babe, in all you say, you are wrong but once; that is, at every point and all simultaneous, like fly-blown carrion. Item: you do protest your age, which is a thing comparative, and with relation to your present company, you're but a bud, an unhatched embryo. Hence we dispose of your fundamental premise, that you have years and wisdom to criticize the way the world is made to wag; which is an enterprise for sound, mature philosophical judgment.

"Item: 'tis evident advantage to everyone, man or moppet, when the world wags smooth. Indeed, whatever tranquillity exists in individual doings is but show and false seeming, like the bark on a rotten apple tree, till those matters that concern the general be at rest. How says Cicero? 'Obedience to reason, which is the law of the universe controlling high and low alike, is the effort by which man realizes his own reason.' Now since there lies a coil between our king and queen that can only be dispersed by the presentation of a changeling from Her Resplendency to His Radiance, the said changeling should take great heart and good cheer at having introduced into the world some portion of harmony that cannot but reflect or exhibit itself in what concerns him more nearly. Now—"

"Yes, but—"

"I crave your grace." He bowed. "Item the third: it is good natural law and justice, too, that you should be chosen. For by old established custom it is demanded of those mortals who have commerce with us that they offer the geld or set out a bowl of milk on St. John's Eve. Now, since your parents failed of this duty, worshipful babe, when snoring Sneckett yonder came he was clearly possessed of the right of leaving an imp or changeling in your room."

"Marry," broke in the winged fairy, "an' that's not all he was possessed of, to bring such a great, ugly hulking creature!"

Scholastic logic, Barber told himself; if this whole queer business were hallucination, this part just might be something his mind had dredged out of the subconscious memory left by college days. There was no use arguing with the old fellow; he'd crawl through a keyhole. No, that way out wouldn't do. However, there was a test that could be applied to the reality of the experience. The senses of touch, hearing, sight could be deceived, but—

"You needn't rub it in," said Barber. "I know I'm no beauty. But I am hungry."

The winged fairy said: "That's a malady we can mend. Who has the bottle?"

A milk bottle with a rubber nipple appeared, and was passed to Butler. He examined it at arm's length for a moment, grinned, pulled off the nipple, and emptied it in a few large gulps. It was milk; he could taste it. Hooray! He felt better. The fairies were murmuring astonishment.

"Thanks," he said, "but I'm still hungry. How about some real food?"

The fairy looked severe. "Sugar-tits have we none. Is't possible you're schooled to sturdier meat?"

"I'll say I am. I'm schooled to bacon and eggs and coffee for breakfast. How about it?"

"Coffee? Oh fraudulent Sneckett! He told us that the folk of your land drank tea."

"They do. I'm just peculiar—lots of ways. I prefer coffee." Barber ground the words a trifle, the suggestion of tea for breakfast capping his annoyance over the constant references to his babyhood. In the service, where one obtained a senior consulship only through white hair and the ability to compare digestive disorders with other old sots, he had been known as "Young" Barber.

Violanta shrugged and spoke into the crowd. A gangling sprite with pointed, hairy ears shuffled up with a tray which contained nothing but a quantity of rose petals.

"What the devil!" exclaimed Barber.

"Your eggs and coffee, sweet babe—or since it's a mortal child, would I say Snookums?"

"Not if you value your health, you wouldn't. And this stuff may look like food to you, but to me it's just posies. I might go for it if I were a rabbit."

"Stretch forth your hand."

He did so; the rose petals turned into a substantial breakfast complete with silver in a recognizable Community pattern. He picked up the coffee cup, sniffed, and peered at it suspiciously. It seemed all right. He squatted on the ground with the tray on his lap and tasted. The result made him gag; it was exactly the rose-flavored coffee served in Hindu restaurants, and a thrill of fear shot through him as he realized this was the perfect pattern of hallucination, the appearance of one thing and the actuality of another.

Violanta caught his expression of dismay. "Your pardon, gracious and most dear Barber-babe," she said, "if the flavor wants perfection. A knavish shaping has turned our spells to naught, and all here have lived on flower leaves since."

"Not very nourishing, I'd say," remarked Barber, sniffing hungrily and remembering that dreadful Yorkshire supper he had toyed with in what now seemed a past a thousand years deep.

"Oh, as to that, fear nothing. 'Twill nourish you featly, though it have the taste of adder's venom."

It might just as well, thought Barber, munching away and trying to forget the heavy, sweet flavor that went with the meal. At least the texture was real enough, indubitably that of bacon and eggs. And the coffee did have the familiar reviving effect of coffee. He finished and laid knife and fork on the tray with a little clink just as the crowned woman came sweeping through the grove again. Barber laid aside the tray and stood up, making the courtliest bow he could manage with a torn pajama-leg dangling around one ankle.

"May I offer my respects to Her Most Resplendent Majesty, Queen Titania?" he said in his best diplomatic manner. "And offer her my services to the small extent of my powers?"

She looked so pleased that her expression became a positive simper. "So young and so well taught!" she said. "I perceive my Violanta has not wasted time. Why, aye; since your offer is fairly made it will be as gladly accepted, and you shall be my messenger of amity before His Radiance. Would that delight you?"

Barber bowed again. "I can't think of anything I'd like better." He might as well, he told himself, play out the string; behave as though this whole crazy business were real and as much a part of his life as, say, the Luftwaffe bombing London. He would have thought that idea crazy, too, if anyone had mentioned it as imminent a year or two back.

"Then let's away," said the Queen. "My coach!"

A wide-mouthed imp, dressed in a blue tabard with an intricate design of silver crescents woven onto it, dropped from the tree branch where he had been sitting and shouted in a voice of surprising volume: "Ho! The Queen's coach!"

Somewhere among the trees another voice took up the cry, then another and another off into the distance, "The Queen's coach! The Queen's coach!" The coach rolled into the glade before the last shout died away, a structure like that used ceremonially by the Lord Mayor of London, if anything more elaborate, more gilded, and drawn by six white horses.

Two footmen leaped down from the tail; Barber noted with a jar of surprise that they were enormous frogs, in appearance and costume duplicates of those Tenniel had drawn for *Alice in Wonderland*. He was diplomat enough not to allow this to upset him, but stepped forward and handed Queen Titania in. She smiled graciously, and opened her mouth to speak, but just at that moment the outrider beside the frog-coachman lifted a trumpet and blew a series of piercing notes. The Queen motioned Barber to join her; he hopped in, the horses started, and they moved off, surrounded by running, flying and shouting fairies. Barber's last glimpse of the glade where he had landed in Fairyland showed him the brownie philosopher, engaged in a startling series of Catherine wheels behind the vehicle.

CHAPTER III

The grove was a mere screen of trees; once through it, they were in an enormous landscaped park where tall blossoms on stalks grew in mathematical precision, interspersed with elms and maples set out in oversize flowerpots. There was no road, but the frog-coachman seemed to know where he was going, and they rolled along easily, coming to a stop with another trumpet flourish and the appearance of the frog-footmen at the door. Barber handed the Queen down.

Behind a row of the flowerpot trees a factory chimney jutted into the air with a yellow-and-blue flag hanging limply from a mast at its peak. "Well met," said the Queen, "His Majesty's in residence at the palace. Come, babe." And she started toward it.

The grass between was set with a maze of fountains, playing high with moon-rainbows through their spray. From one of them a voice suddenly chanted, basso profundo: "Rocked in the cra-a-dul of the de-ee-ee-eep!"

Bombing is notoriously bad for the nerves. Barber jumped, caromed into Queen Titania and both sat down. The water of the fountain heaved itself up into an anthropomorphous shape, like a translucent snow man and stared at him from lidless eyes.

"Blow me down, here's a sniveling mortal!" it boomed. "And rouncing round the Queen! You bag of tripes, I'll better your behavior!" A transparent arm shot out, the fingers clutching for Barber's face. He ducked, threw up a hand to ward the grip, and bumped the Queen again as water splashed all over him. The rest of the aqueous monster subsided into a plain fountain, with a Neptunian bellow: "Ho-ho-ho! Did you see it jump? Haw-haw-haw!"

"Haw-haw-haw!" came an echoing burst of laughter from the other fountains, as the one that had splashed Barber burst into deep-voiced song:

> *"Fifteen men on a dead man's chest,*
> *Yo, ho, ho and a bottle of rum!*
> *Drink and the devil had done for the rest—"*

All the fountains were coming in on the second "Yo, ho, ho—" as Barber scrambled up and offered Titania his hand. She disdained it and leaped to her feet, her good nature gone.

"You clay-headed oaf, you clumsy tallow-ketch!" she blazed in a quietly deadly voice. "Were't not that you are a mere object, a toy for a better man, I'd have you to the strappado! I'll—"

Barber bowed. "A thousand pardons, Your Resplendency! I was only trying—"

She advanced furiously, cocking a fist. "Trying! I'll try you, and in a star-chamber fashion!"

Barber backed, then looked around to make sure he had sea-room, for the living fountains were shouting and singing all around behind him. As he did so his eye caught a figure—a small, thin-haired man in doublet and hose, with a sandy mustache, and a six-inch diamond hanging from a chain around his neck. Titania's eye caught him at the same time as Barber's; she lowered her arm as the man came hurrying up.

"How now?" he said. "Why, it's my sweet cowslip, my pretty helpmate, and with her feathers ruffled like a mourning dove! What—"

"Spare your sarcasms, my lord," snapped the Queen. "Here's your changeling, and good riddance. Now do I get my little Gosh?"

King Oberon looked at Barber. "This great wool-sack jobbernowl a changeling?"

"Aye, and I give you joy of him. Just now the light-some ox strewed my royal dignity upon the path."

"Ha, ha! Would I had seen it. If you dislike him so, the colt must have better points than show in his teeth."

"Why, you starveling stick—" Titania suddenly seemed to recollect that she had come not to quarrel, but to get something she wanted by exchange. Her face underwent a lightning transformation. "In very faith, it's not so useless a wretch; can argue, stretch a point like a philosopher. Will you not take it, give me my Gosh, and set our affairs once more to their wonted smoothness? My lord knows full well there has been another shaping."

The King rubbed his chin. "Full well, indeed. I cast a spell for a hunting lodge and get these cursed, crank living fountains. I'm still not won to your thought that the variance between us lies at the root of these shapings. But 'tis most evident they are there-by increased in effect, like a pox with exercise, since we can receive in our affairs only what we put forth. So, since you wish it, madam, let there be peace be-tween us."

The fairies, who had been crowding around, went into shouts of delight over this announcement, and began the same series of antics Barber had seen them perform before. Titania's smile, though gracious, was a trifle glassy.

"And my little Gosh?" she asked.

Oberon swallowed, then lifted his voice and shouted: "Gosh!" There was no answer. He tried again. Still no response. "Herald!" he called.

A sprite, the twin of the one who had called the Queen's coach, save that his tabard bore a design of suns, somersaulted into position, opened his mouth and shouted: "Chandra Holkar Raghunath Tippu

Vijayanagar Rao Jaswant Rashtrakuta Lallabhbhai Gosh! Come forth, you misbegotten imp, you villainous standing-tuck, you—"

"Here sir," said a dark-skinned boy of about twelve, appearing suddenly. "Did you call, O Pearl of Wisdom?"

"Call? Aye, and for the last time. Take the brat, then, my lady, and let me call myself well shut of him."

Chandra Holkar Raghunath Tippu Vijayanagar Rao Jaswant Rashtrakuta Lallabhbhai Gosh stood grinning unregenerately, with his feet apart and two small thumbs hooked into his sash, then turned to Titania and bowed. "Am I truly to be yours again, O Star of Beauty and Queen of Felicity?"

"Aye," said Titania. "Come, my babe. Let's to our chambers."

The boy winked at Barber. Oberon's mouth suddenly fell open. "It's not to be done," said he.

"And wherefore not?"

"There's a matter—they are not fit—" As he stumbled Barber experienced for the third time, and stronger than ever, the sixth sense that told him the man was lying. But Oberon rushed on: "That is, I did prepare your apartment against your coming and it is but now all betousled and lumbered with new decoration. Since you left my bed—"

"It stayed cold not long, I'll warrant," said Titania, her foot beginning to tap dangerously.

Oberon's fists clenched and the diamond danced on his chest. "Fie! Fah! By Beelzebub's brazen—look you, who are you to talk, wench, with a changeling in your train whose beard sprouts and fists are like footballs! Call me kobbold if he's not good for more games than ring-around-a-rosy." Before Titania could retort, he swung suddenly on Barber. "Sirrah! How long have you known my wife? Quick and true or turn to a frog!"

"If you mean how long since I met the lady," said Barber, his sixth sense warning him there was something phony about this outburst, "maybe an hour. If you mean—"

"Enough, let be. Your reply's ample."

"But not yours to me," said Titania. "Come, Gosh, we'll see what 'tis my lord is so desirous to conceal." She swept regally toward the factory chimney, followed by the boy. Oberon muttered after her. "Wish her joy of her conquest. He's found a taste for felonious magic—oh, a perfect accomplished young cutpurse . . . Yet now what's to do?" He looked wildly from side to side, then seized Barber's arm. "Your name, fellow!"

"Barber."

"Marry, a most proper one to the emergency, since here's a great bloated business to be bled docile. Art trustworthy?" He poked his face close, then went on rapidly: "No matter, it's a case of trust and be damned, or doomed for lack of trust. Harkee, fellow Barber: there be two entrances to my lady's apartment, by the staircase and through our royal rooms. Do you take the nearer while we move with her ladyship by the longer route. Will find a wench there—ha, ha, 'tis a babe of parts, I see you take my meaning. Well, spirit her away; exorcise her, by any means. Come!"

Still gripping Barber's arm, the King went across the grass after Titania in a series of bounds, dragging the other with him. They were together at the entrance to the chimney, which proved to have surprising interior dimensions and a helical staircase that went up and up. "Pox take these villain shapings," panted Oberon, as they climbed, "that will not let us mount by the old Fairyland method of a word and aloft. Ouf!"

He came to a halt on a landing opposite a brown door, and as the other two took the circuit that carried them out of sight, yanked out a key and pressed it into Barber's hand. "So, and nimbly," he whispered, then bounded up the stairs after the Queen.

There seemed no lock or even latch on the door. Wondering why he had been given the key, Barber pushed. He found himself in a kind of sitting room with tapestry-covered benches along the walls wherever they were not cut by archways. Each of the latter led to another room on a different level, some up, some down. He raced from door to door, seeing nothing promising till he reached one that gave on a room

in which an elaborate gold-and-damask four-poster bed
was visible, with another door beyond. That ought to
be it. Barber leaped down a step, past the bed, and
tried the door. No soap.

The key? But this door was as innocent of keyholes
as that on the stairway. Perhaps it was bolted on the
other side. He knocked. The wood emitted a dull
sound, indicative of solidity, but there was no answer.
Using the metal key to make the noise louder, he
knocked again. Instantly the door swung open and
he found himself looking across a wide apartment at
an extremely pretty girl in a thin dress, seated before
a mirror and winding something starry into her hair.
She had wings.

At the sound of Barber's entry she turned a startled
face in his direction. "The Queen!" he said. "Oberon
says for you to clear out."

The girl's mouth fell open, and as it did so there
was the sound of another door somewhere among the
labyrinth of rooms, accompanied by Titania's pene-
trating voice.

The girl leaped from her stool and dashed to a
closet. In a matter of seconds she was out with an
armful of silky garments and a wad of fancy shoes in
one hand, scooting past Barber as he held the door
for her. He pulled it to behind them.

"Lock, quickly!" she said. "You have the key?"

Barber gazed uncomprehendingly from the lockless
door to the instrument he still held clutched in his
hand.

"Ah, stupid!" she cried, and snatching it from his
hand, passed it through the loop-shaped handle, muttering something meanwhile, and turned to examine
him from top to toe. "A changeling babe, I'll warrant,"
she said finally, "else you had not been so ignorant of
means. Even shapings alter not these."

Barber felt a surge of irritation over these continual
references to his babyhood. "I suppose you could call

me a changeling," he replied, a trifle coldly, "but I'm not a baby—by any means. Permit me to present myself. I am Fred Barber, of—" He took a step backward to bow as he made the formal introduction. As he did so the pit of his knee touched the edge of a chair and he went down into it, with no damage but complete loss of dignity.

An expression of surprise flashed over her face and she gave a tittering laugh. "Oh, la, Sir Changeling," she said, "to take advantage of a poor girl so! No babe indeed, but a very Don Cupid. Well—" she put her head on one side and surveyed him brightly, like a bird—"I've played pat-lips with less lovely lords, so let's on."

"Huh?"

The girl dropped her armful of clothes, took two quick steps, and was on Barber's lap, with both arms round his neck. "'Ware my wings," she said. Her hair had a faint perfume.

"Hey!" said Barber, though not at all displeased by the sensations he was experiencing. "What have I done to deserve this?"

Her eyes widened. "Is't possible you are so ignorant, sweet simpleton? Yet I forget—you are a stranger. Why, then, you took a single chair, not a bench nor the floor, nor offered me a place to sit, and we're alone. In the exact custom of our realm, that is to say you wish to play loblolly—oh, shame! And I thought you meant it!" Her face flushed.

There was a knock at the inner door.

"That's Oberon," said Barber. "I really mean it, but—"

"Ho, Barber!" came the King's voice muffled by the door.

"Alack for might-have-been," said the girl, and kissed him.

"Ha, Barber fellow! Open!" came from the door. The girl slid to her feet, gathered her gowns and slippers with a single motion, danced over to the window and leaped lightly to the sill. Barber jumped to his feet, but before he could reach the window she was gone, her gauzy wings glittering on the downbeat in the moonlight. He returned to the door and tapped it with the key. It opened to reveal Oberon talking amicably with Titania and Gosh. "So, a good day, then my love," said the King, "and goodhap."

He bowed, came through and closed the door after him, then clapped Barber lustily on the back. "Well and wisely done, fellow! You have our royal favor. But, hist, take an older man's advice—if you must make merry with our Fairyland doxies, choose one without wings."

"Why?" asked Barber, wondering how much Oberon knew about the incident in the chair, and how he could know.

"Take thought, man. Merely imagine."

"Oh."

"Now then, to the next matter—your garb. It's not fit for the court. Stand here before me."

Oberon made a series of rapid passes with his hands, reciting:

> "One, two, three, four,
> Doublet and hose, such as Huon bore;
> Uno', do', tre', quaro',
> Clothe to warm both flesh and marrow,
> Ichi, ni, san, shi
> Garb him then, as he should be . . ."

Fred Barber felt a soft impact; looked down, and to his utter horror found himself covered with a complete suit of tree frogs—hundreds of them, clinging in a continuous layer by their sucker-toed feet. He yelped and jumped. All the tree frogs jumped too, cascading over the floor, the furniture and the frenzied King, who was bouncing with rage.

"Ten thousand devils!" he shrieked. "Pox, murrain, plague, disaster upon this stinking puke-stocking shaping! I'll—"

Barber recovered first, bowing amid the leaping batrachians, his diplomatic training asserting itself enough to make him remember that distraction was the first step in curing a fury like this. "I beg Your Majesty's pardon for making so much trouble. But if I may trouble you still further, would you explain to me what this shaping is? If I am to serve Your Majesty, it seems I ought to know about it."

Oberon's rage came to a halt in mid-flight. He rubbed his chin. "The curse of our domain, and insult to our sovranty, lad. If with your mortal wit you can do aught to alter them, all favor's yours to the half of the kingdom. Look you—you come from a land where natural law is immutable as the course of the planets. But in our misfortunate realm there's nought fixed; the very rules of life change at times, altogether, without warning and in no certain period. . . . Oh, fear nothing; we'll have the royal tailor in to—"

"And these changes are called shapings?"

"Aye; you have hit it. There's an old prophecy gives us to hope, somewhat about a hero with a red beard, whose coming will change the laws of these laws, but I'm grown rank skeptic in the matter. There is this also, that with each shaping things grow faintly worse, by no more than a mustard seed, d'you understand? Yon fairies in the Queen's train, when once they began playing, hopped happily all night. Now they grow tired, need a new stimulus, which accounts for my lady's humor, who likes joy about her. And here's my great jewel, that before the last shaping had the property of—Why, where's the bauble?"

Oberon looked down at the starry front of his doublet. " 'Tis gone—I know, 'twas that brown fiend, the Hindu cutpurse. I've been robbed! I—the King—robbed in my *royal palace!*" Oberon was hopping around the room like one of the tree frogs. "Devils burn him! Scorpions sting him! Lightning fry him! The sanguine little cheat, the stinking blackguard!"

Barber gave up and put his fingers in his ears. When the torrent had died down a trifle, he removed them and asked, "Why doesn't Your Majesty tan his hide? Sounds as though he needed discipline."

"Discipline him? Titania dotes on him *in extremis,* and he's her ward. I can do nothing, though he intends murder most foul, without oversetting what little law remains in this plagued land. Ah, faugh! Never wear a crown, Barber fellow; 'tis light enough on the brow, but on mind and heart heavy." He yawned. "To bed; get you gone, the third arch by the left if the room's still there after this last foul shaping. An elf will attend you."

Barber left the king unlacing his shoes and singing away to himself quite cheerfully:

> *"But when I came, alas! to wive,*
> *With hey, ho, the wind and the rain;*
> *By swaggering could I never thrive,*
> *For the rain it raineth every day."*

The room was still there, but with neither glass nor curtains to the windows, and the level lines of a morning sun streaming across the floor. Apparently the nocturnal fairies went to sleep as naturally in a glare of sunlight as mortals did in darkness. Barber wondered if he could do the same. He thought maybe he could, having been up all night, and turned back the covers of the enormous silk-covered bed that nearly filled the room. As he lay down it occurred to him that there was something particularly undreamlike in falling asleep in a dream; and that going calmly to sleep was hardly in tune with any form of insanity. This gave him a fine sense of satisfaction in the actuality of the experience that was registering itself on his senses till he remembered that Oberon had described the experience itself as utterly lawless. Even the means of getting back to his own world—if this were the illusion and not that—would presumably be adventitious. Still trying to unravel the logical difficulties this involved, he drifted off.

CHAPTER IV

A gentle clearing of the throat awakened him. The sound went on and on, as diminutive as a mouse's alarm clock. Barber ignored it till he found he would have to turn over anyway, then opened his eyes.

A small, wizened elf with a leather bag in one hand stood by his bed. "Gweed morrow, young sir," said this mannikin. "I'll be the tailor royal. His Radiance bade me attend ye."

Barber slid out of bed, his toes searching futilely for slippers that were not there. The elf whipped a tape measure, its markings spaced unevenly as though an inch were sometimes one length, sometimes another.

"Hm," said the tailor. "Ye're an unco great stirk of a mortal. But I'll fit ye; I'll jacket ye and breek ye and cap ye." He began pulling clothes from the bag—underwear and a shirt and a pair of trunks that bulged around the hips. All went well till Barber began trying on jackets with pinched waists and leg-of-mutton sleeves. His squarish, straight-lined torso had no median joint to speak of. The elf grunted, "Too muckle wame," thrust the largest of the jackets back into the bag, muttered something, and took it out again.

This time the waist was all right, but Barber complained: "It's still tight across the back of the shoulders."

The elf helped him take the jacket off and felt of his shoulder blades. Barber was conscious that the probing fingers touched a little point of no-sensation, like an incipient boil, on each scapula. The tailor whistled. "Heuch! Ye'll be having a rare pair o' wings afore ye're mickle older. I maun make ye a wingity coat."

"*What?*" The weight came back to his mind with a bump, and for a moment he felt bitter at human adaptability, which had deceived him into acceptance of a situation that—contradicted itself. The elf was speaking: "—wear that ane until I get your wingity jacket made. Noo the collar." The tailor pulled from the bag a starched ruff that was probably ten inches in diameter, though it looked thirty.

"Is that a collar or do I wear it around my middle?" demanded Barber.

The wrinkled countenance showed no appreciation of this attempt at humor. "A collar. It buttons tae your sark. It's a coort regulation."

"Oh, well," said Barber. "I've taken off my shoes for the Son of Heaven, worn white tie and tails at noon for the President of the Third Republic, and silk knee-britches in Spain. I guess I can stand it." The tailor put the ruff on him, standing on tiptoe to button it. "How the devil do you eat in one of these things?"

"Tip your head weel forward, and 'ware the gravy."

A flat cloth cap with a stiff brim all round came out of the bag and went on a table beside the bed. The elfin tailor whipped out a metal mirror and held it up before Barber, who surveyed himself with satisfaction and the thought that Francis Drake must have looked like that. He turned to the tailor. "What's your name?"

"Angus, sir."

"How old are you, Angus?" (If he could keep talking, plunge himself deeply enough in the objective world, however irrational that objective world might at the moment seem, the real, rational world in which he was actually living must break through to the level of consciousness.)

"Twelve hundred and fifty, sir."

Once more, stronger than ever, Barber experienced the sensation of being in the presence of a lie. He grinned: "How old are you really, Angus?"

The respectful look became a grimace of uneasiness. "Weel, your young lairdship mustna gie me awa, but

I'll be fifteen hundred and ninety-ane years auld, come—"

"That's all right. You don't look a day over a thousand." The small victory gave Barber a comforting sense of superiority. "Suppose you tell me something about this country. What are we bounded by?"

"Fat's that?"

"What's north of here? Ditto with east, south and west."

"That depends on which way north is, sir. Maist times, 'tis straight up. The last time 'twere doon, 'twas in the direction of the Kobold Hills."

"And what are the Kobold Hills?"

Angus shifted his feet and tucked the mirror into his jerkin, where it disappeared without leaving a bulge. "The hills where the kobolds be," he said.

"Who are the kobolds?" (Fairies of some sort, he remembered from youth, but the word might have a special meaning.)

"I dinna really ken, sir." His eyes avoided; the falsehood was so obvious that the elf himself felt it. "If your clothes are satisfactory, sir, I'll tak my leave." Without waiting for more he whisked out of the room.

Barber called after him: "How about a razor—" but too late. A fingertip assured him of the stubble on his chin, but none of the furniture contained anything that was the least use in such an emergency, so he shrugged and went into the entry hall to look for the King.

The archway to the royal rooms showed nothing, but from another came the sound of voices and Barber rightly guessed this must be the breakfast room. It was long and high-ceilinged, with huge, arched glassless windows—didn't it ever rain or get cold here, he wondered?—and the astonishing bright moonlight of fairyland streaming in. He was conscious of fantastic polychrome decoration and piled glass chandeliers that must be utterly useless amid the regular procession of sunlight-moonlight. But the center of his eye was taken up by the table and its occupants.

It was twenty feet or more long, covered with a damask cloth that dripped to the floor, and from the far end Titania faced him, regal and smiling. Behind her stood Gosh and the brownie philosopher; uniformed footmen bustled about. At the other end, with his back to Barber, sat Oberon, also with two attendants. The King had just finished eating something; one of the footmen whisked a gold plate from under his nose, and four tall goblins with spindling legs and huge puffed cheeks, standing stiffly midway down the table, lifted silver trumpets and blew. Their music was like that Barber had heard from the gallery at the coronation of George VI.

Titania had seen him and indicated his direction through the music with a wave of her hand. Oberon turned. "Ho, it's the Barber fellow!" he cried. "Ha, slugabed! Approach, approach."

Another dish had appeared before him. He transferred part of the contents to a plate and handed it to a footman. "To Barber, with our royal compliments," he said. Instantly one of the trumpeters blew a blast like an elaborated version of an army mess call. The footman's nose was flattened back till it resembled a pig's snout, and he had prick ears that pointed like the horns of a cow as he bowed before Barber.

"You're in high favor, Sir Changeling," he whispered quickly, handing over the plate. "Speak a word for me about the pixie Amaranthe; I'll do as much for you one day. I am called Gryll."

"Will if I can," answered Barber out of the corner of his mouth and bowed toward Oberon, who was watching him. He looked around for a chair. There were none in the room except those occupied by the King and Queen, so he supposed he would have to eat standing up. The food was pale blue in color and strongly flavored with violet; Barber, who had never

been able to get used to the English habit of sweets
with breakfast, found it perfectly abominable. Fortu-
nately, he was spared the worst effects of the King's
generosity, for no sooner had he taken a couple of
mouthfuls than Oberon was beckoning him to the
table.

"Harkee, Barber," he said. "You're a fine springald;
full of inches, thewed like an ox, and with a heart
of oak, I'll warrant. Is't not so?"

Barber bowed and managed to get rid of the plate
of blue goo. "Your Radiance is too kind." This was
like being in the service; when they wanted something from you they always began by spreading the
oil good and thick.

"If you're as kind to our wishes you shall ride high
in our favor. We have a deed to lay on you, a com-
mission to execute—"

Whatever else he was going to say was drowned in
another outburst from the goblin trumpeters. Titania
had changed plates. Oberon's face writhed, he brought
his fist down on the table, but the Queen was quicker
in catching the precise moment when the tooting
stopped.

"My very dear lord and gossip," her bell-like voice
rang out, "you do forget your guest. A wight that
casts his shadow wants nourishing." She handed a
plate to one of her footmen. "Our royal compliments
to Master Barber, and may he prefer this to the last
dish." He did; it tasted like steak.

Oberon slapped his forehead with an open palm.
"Oh, apologies, Barber; we crave your grace. Now on
the matter of this achievement: it's the kobolds."

"What about them?" asked Barber, munching away.

"We fear they're making swords again to ruinously
vex our realm. The beat of forging hammers comes
from their hills, and has a droll ring to it, as though
they were not working good honest bronze but—iron."

He let the last word drop slowly; as he did so the footmen started and one of them dropped a plate.

"I still don't see—"

"Why, halt 'em, thwart 'em, confound their knavery! You're mortal; plainly you can handle the stuff."

The brownie philosopher at the other end of the table was bowing like a jack-in-the-box. Titania said: "You have our permission. For two minutes only, though."

"Gracious lord, gracious lady," he piped. " 'Tis clear to my arts that this changeling stands before you uncomprehending, like a bull in a buttery. What's to do, a asks, and Your Radiance but gives him commands, when it's a sapient babe that will see to the heart of the millstone."

He bowed to Barber and squeaked on: "These kobolds are a race that consort not with us, loving labor like Egyptians. Yet we would not be without them, for they are natural like ourselves, and how says Protagoras: 'All things in nature are good and have their place; and if the least attractive be removed the lack will ultimately be felt by all.' Which I take it to be—"

"Ahem!" said Oberon loudly.

The brownie philosopher bowed three times, hurriedly. "Now the minds of these kobold-cattle are so fashioned that since they alone, of all Fairyland, have the power of touching iron, they make of fashioning that metal an inordinate vainglory, preferring it to all others—"

Titania silently held up two fingers.

"Yes, gracious lady. . . . And would therefore forge swords at every opportunity. Which swords, being distributed, do set all Fairyland at the most horrid strife and variance, with bloodletting and frequent resultant shapings—"

Bang! Oberon's fist came down. "A truce to babble!

Here's the riddle: we of pure fairy blood cannot go to the Kobold Hills, which stink of the curst metal. Thus you're our emissary."

Barber's ears had caught the slight accent on the word "pure." "Because I'm of impure fairy blood, I suppose?" he questioned lightly.

"Wherefore else, good Barber?"

He laughed, but it died out against the unaltered faces around him. "Who was your mother's mother, sir?" asked Titania's clear contralto.

"I . . . don't know." He had always assumed he had two grandmothers, like everyone else. They came in pairs. But looking up family trees had always struck him as a sport that led either to the D.A.R. or the booby hatch, places he was equally anxious to avoid. Oberon pressed against his confusion.

"There are brooks also since the last shaping—plagued ungainly obstacles to us of the pure blood, who must seek round by their sources or fly high above, but not for you, mortal. Go, then, we say; be our embassy, our spy."

"And if I do, can I get back to where I came from? After all, I have work—"

"Why, you unhatched egg, you chick-cuckoo, will you bargain against the King's Radiance of Fairyland? Go to! I'll—"

The brownie philosopher was wriggling in a perfect passion of desire for speech, but Titania signed him to silence and Oberon, catching sight of the motion, pulled himself up short. "Ha!" he said. "I misremember; 'tis long since we had a new changeling. Why, good Barber, the rule of our realm touching mortals is this: none is brought here but for some weighty enterprise. Which accomplished, he's free to return."

"And mine is to keep your kobolds from making swords?"

"Perhaps." (That isn't true, Barber's developing

sixth sense flashed to him.) "Ask Imponens there; he's sib to such secrets of nature."

"But not to this, my lord." The brownie philosopher exhaled a long breath at being allowed to speak and fingered his beard. "No more than you or the change-ling himself can I tell such reasons; and that is, I hold, the nature of life in all worlds, as I shall reveal by a most philosophical question. Tell me, Sir Babe, an you know—why were you born into the world you came from?"

"I—" began Barber, confused by this sudden change in the plane of the discussion.

"You would say, pure chance. To which I reply: No, not no more than the step by which you were brought here. For Chance is but the cipher of a power that does not wish to sign its name. . . . You see, I follow your thought like a slothound; 'tis my art, of which each of us here, mortal or fairy, has one, even as in the world you came from each has some little talent. . . . Ha! Your Radiance, Your Resplendency!" He bowed rapidly toward one end of the table and then the other. " 'Ware this changeling lad, I say. I have hunted his aptitude to its lair as he thought on't but now. He'll set your court by the ears, for he can tell lies from truth whenever spoken."

Oberon leaned back in his chair and unexpectedly burst into laughter. All the footmen, butlers and gob-lin trumpeters obediently imitated him, and as one of the latter laughed a series of bubbling toots into his instrument got Barber himself to laughing. Only Ti-tania and Gosh kept their composure. He noticed that the latter was making a rapid series of passes with his hands and moving his lips. The mound of blue on Oberon's plate vanished; the boy chewed and swal-lowed.

"Ho-ho, 'tis rare, rank rare," gasped Oberon, com-ing out of his laughing fit by degrees. "Well, my pretty cosset, how think you now on your bargain? You have your little felon, ha-ha, but I've gained me a counselor that shall make you both jig a step or two. Tell me, good Barber, what is your profession?"

"I was in the diplomatic service."

"There 'tis; those who gain a faculty by commerce with us get generally one that would be most useful whence they came. Though meseems 'twould have been nearer the eye to have the power of making your own lies believed."

Titania smiled, only half ruefully. "Then all's well, my lord, if Imponens has but justly judged. It's a sharp archer indeed that never misses the heart."

Oberon had picked up his fork as she spoke and now his eye fell on the empty plate before him. "We'll put it to the proof," he said, and pointed at Gosh. "You whoreson imp! Did you beguile my breakfast but now? Mark his answer, good Barber."

The dark little face took on an expression of bland impudence. "Oh, Gem of Glory," he began, but Titania came to his rescue:

"My noble lord, do we not but bandy while our sovran purpose waits? Here's this Barber, an approved ambassador, whom we are anxious to speed, yet we sit jousting in wind like a pair of sguittards. . . . Gosh! My magic wand; I left it in the apartment. Our messenger shall bear it."

The boy strolled toward one of the doors with his nose in the air and an expression of nonchalance. As he passed the King, Oberon growled: "Beat it hence, you bepuked little mandrake!" but it was covered from Titania's attention by Barber's own remark:

"How am I supposed to use this wand?"

"That," said the Queen, "is something you must learn by experience; no other teacher."

"Aye," added Oberon, "and mark well, Barber; whatever happens, use no physical force against the kobolds."

"Why not?"

"You're outnumbered, one to a thousand. Yet there's a better reason, however high your heart run; these wights are of such nature that they be held under certain bonds against passing to open violence. But if it be first used on them, they are released and can reply in overweening measure. No striking, then; sheer skill."

"But," cried Barber, "you want me to stop them from making swords, but I can't use force. You won't tell me what to do or how to use even the wand."

"You named yourself diplomat, not we. Sure, you're a poor stick in the profession an you have not met such tasks before. . . . Ha, here's the wand."

He took it from Gosh and handed it to Barber. It did not look in the least as it had when Titania used it on Sneckett the evening before, but like an ivory walking stick. The handle end came round in a crook with a carved snake's-head terminal.

"Watch it well," warned Titania. "This wand has an enchantment in it; if it be lost, all concerned including your sweet self will come on some misadventured piteous overthrow. Go, then, and good luck with you."

CHAPTER V

Nothing was easy. The park, with its fantastic potted trees and eight-foot blossoms, stretched farther from the tower than Barber had imagined; and his mind ran round and round the idea Imponens had thrown out, as though at once seeking some escape and happy at not finding it. In midnight arguments that flowered over the third Scotch-and-soda he was used to describing himself as a rational materialist. Like many intelligent people for whom the gospel of St. Einstein had replaced that according to St. John, he read the newspaper science columns and suspected even Jeans and Millikan of transcendentalism. Evidence that could be perceived by the physical senses—everything depended on that. Extrapolation from such evidence was dangerous. It resulted in theory which demanded experimental proof.

It was like reassembling a clock and having it run perfectly with six cogwheels left out to find the evidence on which he had always relied supporting the theory he had always despised. Every physical sense assured him that he was not insane. So did experimental proof, so far as he had been able to make it. And—final piece of conviction!—insane people never considered the possibility that their senses were playing them false.

Yet Fred Barber's senses were assuring him in the most decided fashion that he had been born—that was the only word for it—into another world. Imponens.

had made the only and obvious deduction . . . as he strode along, the picture of that brownie philosopher turning cartwheels came to him and he smiled. It was the last sight he had seen as he left the palace, Imponens cartwheeling through the trees.

His logic cartwheeled too, but always about that only possible deduction. Other worlds stretched beyond this one into the personal future of Fred Barber, which he would enter when he had accomplished his unknown task. But if the future, then the past—he must have come into his own world, the "real" world, from some other still, with a wiping out of memory during the process. Or would memory be wiped out? Barber tried to recall something from the past that might lie behind his conscious past. Was there not something vaguely familiar about the court and its ceremonial?

Hold hard. This was reincarnation. Buddhism. Bahai. Theosophy, and goofy cults presided over by fat ladies with faint mustaches. Barber looked round and found that the tower of the royal palace, which he had been using as a point of departure, was no longer visible. Nobody there had been able to give him any sensible directions to the Kobold Hills. "Take the path and ask as you go," they had said. "The wand will help you."

What path? There were a dozen or a million winding away through the trees to a region of hedges, where the tracks were marked only by a brighter green in the short lawn grass. All curved, rapidly or imperceptibly, and the only comfort was that none of them led to blind alleys. Whenever the hedges seemed about to close him in, there was always a sudden turn, another rank of giant flowers and a new vista. But none of these vistas led to any sign of habitation; down none of them was there visible any life other than botanical. Ask whom as you go?

Yet at this point it looked as though he would have

to ask somebody soon. The path, narrowed to an alley by parallel hedges, flowed into an opening filled with a round bed of the huge flowers. Beyond hedges closed in again, smoothly green, joining the flower bed at its back, so that he must definitely choose between turning right or left. The grass gave no clue; both directions showed the high color that had hitherto been his guide. Everything was still as the moon itself, flooding the scene with cold light, not a sound, not a motion, not a sign of breeze.

"Hey!" said Fred Barber.

No answer. Not an echo either; the foliage seemed to muffle his shout.

The indifference of this landscape had become nerve-racking. He addressed a zinnia the size of a cabbage on a stalk towering over his head: "I wish you could tell me which way to the Kobold Hills," he said aloud.

The blossoms showed no intention of doing so. Damn this whole business! Unfair. His mind abruptly vaulted back to the incident at college when somebody had blown sneeze powder through the old-fashioned hot-air inlet into the room where the faculty dinner was being held. Very funny, but not for Fred Barber, who was student president, and knew that the priceless young fool who did it would get the whole college confined to campus in Junior Week if he didn't own up. He swung the ivory wand up and pointed accusingly at the zinnia:

"Confound it, can't you see you're just making it tough for all of us without helping yourself? Which of these paths goes to the Kobold Hills?"

The zinnia courteously bowed its head toward the path on the right. Barber gazed at the other flowers in the bed; there was still no wind, not a leaf had rustled, not another flower-head changed. He pointed the stick at a bachelor-button the size of a ten-gallon hat: "Do you agree?" he demanded.

The huge flower returned his stare, immobile and impassive. Experimental proof was wanting; and though he turned down the right-hand curve (since there was nothing better to do) the dismaying thought occurred to him that it might always be wanting from the set of circumstances or form of life in which he inexplicably found himself. What was it Oberon had said about shapings? "The very rules of life change—" But if they changed, then there were no rules; life was chaotic. No, wait, life here didn't abandon rules, it shifted unreasonably from one set to another . . .

His shoulder blades itched in unscratchable places. He stopped and reached around with the crook of the walking stick-wand, and could plainly feel the bumps that Angus had informed him were incipient wings. Fred Barber with wings. He tried to picture to himself the commotion at the Embassy if he walked in on them with a pair of great feathered appendages springing from his shoulders. He could imagine old Layton babbling at the sight, with his smug face of a satisfied sheep. And would an authentic winged man have precedence at dinner over a Yugoslav military attaché? If he knew his embassies, the question ought to be good for at least eight hours of argument.

Well, he was out of that now, perhaps permanently, and just ahead of him the hedges were falling away to side and side from another crotch in the road. Between the two forks were flowers, mingled with a perfect forest of the potted trees, and in front of them a man, or at least an individual, was standing on his head. The head was a large one, and the individual seemed perfectly comfortable, with arms and legs folded. At the sound of Barber's footfall he opened a large green eye.

"Beg pardon," said Barber, "but could you direct me to the Kobold Hills?"

The individual said: "What do you want to go there for?"

"Public business," said Barber, trying to make it sound important.

The individual yawned—it looked extremely odd in his position—and opened a second eye. "Not an original remark, my friend. You're the—let's see—forty-ninth mortal to go through here. They're always on public business. Forty-nine is seven times nine. I wouldn't go any farther."

"Your arithmetic's wrong and whether I go or not is my business. How do I get there?"

The individual opened a third eye in the middle of his forehead. "No it isn't. It's only mortal affection for exact systems that makes you say that. I know all about Oberon's monkey business with the kobolds. It's a waste of time. And you're mistaken about those colors. They call them greengrocers because they feel blue."

Barber had a sensation of trying to wade through mud, but clung manfully to the main issue. "Why is it a waste of time to do anything about the kobolds? They'll make trouble if they're not stopped, won't they?"

The individual closed two of his eyes. "Lots of trouble," he said cheerfully. "They'll lay the country waste. Your development is incomplete. You can't follow more than one line of reasoning at a time. That makes for errors."

"Then what's the objection to thwarting them?"

"It's an inevitable transition stage before we can have anything better. If your development were complete you'd see that the kobolds were destined to sweep away the old corrupt order."

"What's corrupt about it?"

"So that's your line, is it? Very well, do you admit that perfection exists?"

"We—ell," said Barber doubtfully, "there's a word for it, so I suppose that in a sense—"

"Either a thing exists or it doesn't. If it exists in a sense it exists in all senses. Just as you're made not less a man by being an outsize, humpbacked mortal man."

"Go on," said Barber.

"Now, if it exists it is patently worth striving for, isn't it?"

"I'll concede that for the moment."

"Fine. Now I'm sure you'll admit that Oberon is not perfect. He quarrels with his wife and keeps winged fairies in the bedroom while she's away."

"I suppose you could hardly call that perfection."

"Aha! Then since perfection is worth striving for, Oberon, being imperfect, is not worth striving for. He is corrupt and should be swept away. Q.E.D."

"But will the kobolds produce perfection?"

"Far more of it than Oberon. They outnumber him, a thousand to one, d'you see? Even if the unit quantity of perfection per individual were far lower, the total mass would work out higher."

"Listen," said Barber, in some exasperation. "I'd like to stand here and split hairs with you all night, but I've got a job to do. Which way to the Kobold Hills?"

"Then you admit I'm right?"

"I'll admit anything if I can be on my way."

"Then," said the inverted person calmly, "by admitting I'm right you admit implicitly that you are wrong. Therefore you don't want to go to the Kobold Hills."

"All the same I'm going. Which way?"

The remaining eye closed wearily, and the voice sank to a mumble. "Either one you like—or—perhaps both—yes, I think—you'd better take—both."

Barber turned away and trudged resolutely down the left-hand fork, reflecting that he had taken the right at the last choice. Since there seemed no rules of sequence in this experience, he would probably come out nearest correct by doing exactly the opposite of what had been successful before. The way seemed clear enough in this direction, though a little beyond Three-eyes and his fork hedges closed in from both sides again and it wound round in the familiar involutions. Barber followed it around a sweeping curve, up a slope—and found himself approaching a fork whose center was occupied by a flower bed with trees behind. In front of the flowers an individual was standing on his head.

"I told you it was no use," he remarked as Barber came up to him. "You don't really want to go to the Kobold Hills."

"Oh, yes, I do. I took the wrong fork last time, no thanks to you, but I'm going to take the other one this time." Barber stepped resolutely to the right.

Two of the green eyes came open. "Just a minute. It's only fair to warn you, my friend, that if you turn to the right, you'll come back here just the same. The way's longer and more fatiguing though. Better go to the left again; you'll get here quicker."

Barber ignored him and strode resolutely down the right-hand path. After a little distance, however, he was obliged to admit that Three-eyes had been right about one thing, at least. The path here was certainly more fatiguing. It climbed sharply; his foot struck an outcrop of rock. He looked down; instead of the lawn-like carpet on which he had been walking, the path underfoot was now nearly bare, except for rank tufts of yellowish vegetation, and ahead the rocks were more frequent. The hedges had changed character here, too. They were much taller, at least twenty feet, and had come in close to pinch the path to a mere passage. The turns, too, were no longer rounded curves but angles; and as Barber negotiated one of them, something caught and scraped across the back of his hand, leaving a scratch that showed little drops of blood. The hedges here had thorns.

He climbed. At a little summit the hedge on one side broke back to reveal a sandy depression. In the middle of it, a few yards from the path, was another native, with a long, horsy face, elaborately rigged out in some sort of tweedy material with a red silk sash sweeping diagonally down across his chest. He had a crooked stick in both hands and was violently banging it into the sand, throwing up little spurts with each stroke.

"Hello," said Barber.

The native glanced up, revealing a monocle on his face, swung the stick over his shoulder and brought it down again—swish-thump! "Thirty-four, sixty-two," said the native as a grain of sand landed in Barber's eye.

"Sorry," said the native curtly, shifted his feet, and drove the stick down again, so the next explosion of sand went off in another direction. "Thirty-five, sixty-seven," he remarked to himself.

Barber extracted the grain of sand, and asked: "Beg pardon, but can you tell me the way to the Kobold Hills?"

Swish-thump! "Thirty-three, sixty-one."

Barber raised his voice: "Hey, can you tell me—"

The monocled face swung round like a gun turret. "My good mortal, I'm not deaf."

"Then why don't you answer?"

"Can't."

"Oh, you mean you don't know."

"Certainly I know. But I can't tell you."

"Why not?"

"Because I don't know you. We haven't been introduced. You might be some blighter."

Barber hovered between laughter and annoyance and compromised on a snort. "Look here," he said, "I'm on state business." He shook the wand. "Here's my credentials. Now suppose you—"

"No use, old thing. Awfully sorry and all that. Nothing personal."

"But it's important!"

"Oh, undoubtedly; I quite understand. Safety of the realm and all that." He elevated one hand and pointed the index finger at his forehead. "Ah, I have it! You find old Jib; lives down the road a bit. Literary chap, so it doesn't matter whom he meets. He can make the introductions." He showed Barber a tweedy shoulder and swung again. "Forty-one, fifty-eight."

The hedge-lined track plunged down sharply, angled, angled again, changed character to the original type of hedge-and-grass within a couple of hundred yards, and Barber found himself back at the fork in the roads, with the inverted sophist regarding him out of one green eye.

"You're beginning to develop. Now that you perceive the compelling logic of the situation, why not take the next step?" he said. "Give up this trip and align yourself with the forces of progress. A little temporary violence is necessary to achieve any great improvement."

Barber gripped the ivory wand and advanced grimly on Three-eyes. "Look here," he said, "I'm going to the Kobold Hills and if you don't tell me how to get there, there's going to be a little temporary violence right now."

The individual raised all three eyebrows—or, rather, lowered them, being upside down. "Are you threatening me, mortal?"

"You're damn'd right, I'm threatening you!"

"Evidently you will accomplish nothing against the kobolds."

"Why not?"

"The complaint is the manufacture and use of instruments of force, is it not? It's the one that hidebound old nympholept Oberon usually makes."

"Yes," admitted Barber, drawn back into the argument in spite of himself.

"To prevent them," said Three-eyes triumphantly, "it is necessary for you to use an instrument of force on me. You thus adopt the methods of the kobolds. In the higher sense, which looks beyond externals, you *are* a kobold. Therefore, you cannot thwart them, be-

cause you would be thwarting yourself in the process.
Q.E.D. OUCH!"

Barber had jabbed at him with the point of the
wand, but before it made contact with the comfortable
belly that instrument gave off a long streak of blue
fire. It touched Three-eyes and ran all over him, leaving him shining with a phosphorescent light. The
mouth flew open and the creature gasped:

"All right, I'll tell you. Take that thing away. I'm
an elemental force. You can't get away from me till
you propose a problem for which I can't find a logical
solution. . . . But I don't think you can do that," he
added as Barber lowered the wand. "Mortals lack a
sense of process." A smile of self-satisfaction spread
across the inverted countenance. "Don't try Achilles
and the tortoise on me; I know that one."

Barber fingered his chin in puzzlement, considering
the question. There was no reaction from his newly
developed instinct for lies; presumably this singular
creature was perfectly right when he said he would
have to be outargued. Yet how to do that? . . . His
fingers revealed a pronounced stubble of beard, far
more than he should have grown in two nights and
a day. This was presumably another characteristic of
Fairyland—that it made his whiskers grow unreasonably. It certainly needed the attention of either a barber or a Barber with a razor, which reminded him of
being called *ad nauseam*, "The Barber of Seville."

Three-eyes, who had shut all of them, opened one.
"I thought so," he remarked. "Better give it up."

Barber of Seville! That was it—Bertrand Russell's
paradox of the Spanish barber.

"By no means," he said. "Listen: suppose there's a
village in Spain which nobody enters or leaves. In
this village there is one barber, male and clean-shaven.
If this barber shaves every man in the village who does
not shave himself; if he does *not* shave any man in

the village who does shave himself: who shaves the barber?"

"I should have mentioned that mortals who try to stick me and fail generally turn into parasites of some kind," said the creature. "Want to withdraw the question?"

"I'll take my chances," said Barber, gripping the wand firmly. It ought to be some protection.

"All right then." The eyes closed. "Let's see—if he does shave himself—by Hecate, then he doesn't—and if he doesn't, he does—"

Barber turned, shaken with inward amusement. As he did so, the now-declining moon threw a new shadow along the hedge at the right. There was a narrow gap in it that he had not noticed before, and the brighter green of the grass in that direction showed a path led through it. He turned into it; a long graceful curve swept away before him, but he had not followed it for more than twenty steps before a vivid blue flash from the direction of the crossroad paled the moon-glow. *Boom!* The shock of an explosion almost took him off his feet.

When his eyes recovered from the glare, he walked quickly back to the gap in the hedge. Three-eyes had vanished.

Barber turned back, and saw he was going down a gentle declivity toward a structure that resembled a large metal hatbox. It had low windows all round, and a faint purring, as of machinery, came from within. In front of it, a bald and burly brown elf was squatted on the grass. His left hand held open the pages of a book. An intricate system of flying trusses composed of small branches had been rigged to one of the potted trees just beside him to hold a cage containing half a dozen fireflies. Presumably they were to furnish light for his reading, but the solid bottom to the cage prevented this from being altogether a success. The elf did not appear to mind. His lips were moving rapidly as he followed the text, and with his other hand he was busily writing something on several sheets of paper, without noticing that his pen had run dry and was leaving no marks whatever.

"Pardon me," said Barber. "Is your name Jib, by any chance?"

"Yes, yes," said the elf. "What can I do for you? Quick, now; I'm writing down my thoughts about this book. I believe it will be my most important work."

"Oh, I'm sorry to interrupt you. Do you know the way to the Kobold Hills?"

"No, no, not now. I used to, but I haven't kept up with athletics recently. I have so much to do in directing the currents of intellectual opinion. You really must read my commentary on this book. It's about the theory of inverse value."

"Would you mind stepping along to introduce me to a fellow with a red sash who doesn't talk to strangers?"

"Yes, yes, surely. Very glad to. The author's theory is sound, but he makes several slight mistakes in arriving at the rationale of inverse values, with the result that he reaches the correct result by the wrong route. My commentary will clarify the whole matter."

"What whole matter?"

"Why, the theory of inverse values," said the elf, tucking the volume under his arm and joining Barber in the path. "We can prove that nothing has any value."

"Huh?"

"Certainly. Obviously two oranges are worth twice as much as one orange."

"I suppose so."

"And one is worth half as much as two. That is, value is proportionate to quantity."

There seemed nothing to do but humor this helpful but argumentative sprite. "I see," said Barber.

"But as quantity approaches infinity, value becomes inverted. A thousand cubic feet of air has no value. The amount of air is, practically speaking, infinite. But if the amount of oranges in Fairyland were infinite? Suppose that, I say, suppose it."

"I am supposing it. What then?"

"Well, an orange is a fruit. You add to the amount of oranges in existence that of lemons, pomegranates, quinces, apples, et cetera, all the fruits that have a supposititious value. The result is a total practically infinite, as in the case of air. Therefore, all these fruits taken together must have an inverse value, or none at all, as in the case of air. And if the total sum has no value, the individual fractions—single oranges, for instance—have no value likewise. . . . The last part is my commentary."

"Beg pardon," said Barber, "but isn't there a flaw in your reasoning?"

"Not at all, not at all, my dear fellow. Mechanically perfect. Cured my orbulina. Here's Cyril now." They had climbed out of the declivity, and Barber saw the same fairy, whacking away and muttering, "Forty-four, eighteen." Evidently they were on the opposite side of his clearing than Barber had approached before; he could see the tall thorn hedges beyond.

"What's your name?" demanded Jib. "Barber? I say, Cyril! I want you to meet my old friend Barber."

"Right-ho," said the tweedy native, with energetic cordiality. "Delighted, charmed. How can I help you?"

Barber repeated the now-wearisome question.

"Oh, surely," said Cyril. "Only too glad. Keep right along this path, but—let's see, this is Monday, what? Then you have to take the left fork at the first turning. Carry right on till you reach *the* forest. You'll have to ask your way after you get into it, I'm afraid. The shapings do things to the forest paths. Look here, do you want me to accompany you?"

"It might be helpful, but aren't you busy?"

"Well, rather. I'm just on the edge of setting a new record. But for a friend of old Jib's . . ."

"Oh, I wouldn't think of bothering you, then. What do you mean by *the* forest?"

"There are forests and forests. This is *the* forest. Cheerio, then."

He shook hands, and turned to thumping at the sand again. Jib squatted down with his book on his knees, and began to go through the motions of writing, oblivious of the fact that he had left both the inkless pen and his paper behind.

CHAPTER VI

Meandering ahead the path took a slight downward slope and the hedges opened out to reveal a new and monotonous succession of flower beds. To Barber, trying to gain some sense of the geography of the place for a homeward journey he supposed he would have to make in time, it seemed that he was going in exactly the same direction as that which had carried him past Cyril and back to the fork where Three-eyes held forth. He cursed a faulty sense of orientation and craned his neck to catch a glimpse of the thorn hedges, but a grove of impossible potted elms cut them off, if, indeed, they were there at all.

Carry on.

There were long shadows across the path that hinted of a setting moon. Barber was reminded that he had been walking all night without food. He was not hungry yet, for that matter, but if he were going to eat at all it had better be now. When Oberon's royal chamberlain had handed him one of the ever-filled foodbags carried by Fairyland travelers, it was with the warning that he had better use it before sunrise. A single shaft of sunlight striking the thing was liable to cause a kind of minor shaping. "I mind me well," the chamberlain added in a low voice, "of the bag our gracious lady and Resplendency took on her journey to the Marshes of Meraa. 'Tis no disrespect to mark that she's of careless habit; let the dawn beams on't. Ho! The thing physicked her preciously with a fine reducing diet—carrots uncooked, salads, and wee brown biscuits." Barber had no difficulty in imagining Titania faced with a situation like that; the explosion would—make the bombing of Bradford look weak. The bombing which seemed as remote now as the discovery of the North Pole.

He brushed the crumbs from his lap and stood up. The shadows had lengthened and run together as he ate, the moon was a cooky with a piece bitten out, at the very edge of the horizon. There was still no sign of the sun that had driven away the previous night's moon; perhaps even the ephemerides of Fairyland did not run on schedule. In the weakened light the path was harder to trace. He strained forward to follow it . . . and was swallowed in a dark as intense as though he had suddenly gone blind.

Something slightly chilly brushed past his face from overhead, and he felt a rush of the most horrible fear. To stand there in dark worse than a London blackout and be struck at from above! Something else tapped him gently on one shoulder, like a falling leaf or an insect, and his mind began to fill with pictures of giant winged spiders. He brushed at the shoulder—nothing, and the something touched his leg. All around were sounds and soft whisperings. Fred Barber jumped and would have run—but where? in that maze of hedges and unknown traps. He would have given anything, done anything, to be back at the Adelphi with the air-raid alarm screaming and the Heinkels coming over. This was worse than being bombed, worse than lying in the hospital with a head wound, wondering if you were going nuts, worse than—

Without any preliminary graying of the sky a big red sun jumped up and flooded the whole queer, smiling landscape with light. Another touch came on Barber's hand; he looked down and saw it damp with a big drop of simple rain, and between him and the sun were the slanting silvery lines of a shower.

Barber laughed, too happy with relief to feel shame, and looked up. There was not a cloud in the sky. The rain was coming out of nowhere, faster now, and making a gorgeous triple rainbow against the coming day. He would be soaked—but what of it? The path curved clear before him and he stepped out along it, twirling the wand. When it reached the top of its arc, the rain, though coming faster than ever, didn't seem to strike him. He experimented a little, and discovered that when he held the wand point up it deflected the rain from a circle quite big enough to keep him dry. A practical piece of magic; but he was getting tired, and the rather heavy meal he had taken from the chamberlain's bag made him sleepy.

Besides, it was not very likely that he would find any more natives abroad from whom he could obtain directions. Better rest up. He trotted over to the nearest hedge, rolled under its spread on the cushiony grass, and fixed the wand, point up, among the branches, to keep him dry. Just as he drifted off to sleep, he heard the pattering raindrops cease.

When he woke it was to find the sun already low, the moon up and challenging it. A few minutes brought him to a fork which must be the one Cyril had mentioned. Go left, he had said, since the day was Monday; a piece of reasoning which struck Barber as so characteristic of the place that he stood for a moment wondering whether it was still Monday and, if not, which was the right direction. Finally deciding Cyril would have made allowance for the lapse in time, he took the left fork. The way led down and round a long curve; climbed a steepish rise, and brought him out on the crest of a low hill, with a broad meadow between him and a dark wall of midnight green—*the* forest, so denominated. The sun was down behind it.

Fred Barber took a long breath and marched resolutely across the meadow into the encroaching gloom under the branches. He could feel the gentle strain at the back of his jacket where the little bulges that must really be wings pulled against it, and there seemed to be a new set of muscles developing at his chest.

The forest was one of large trees, old as time, with neither grass nor underbrush around their trunks. It would be like the tame parked forests of Germany, Barber thought, but for the bulging of knots and scars, which in the tricky moonlight gave almost every tree some semblance of a human face. A scowling eye greeted him from the gloom ahead, a mournfully drooping mouth followed him there.

Overhead spots of sky were scattered beyond the leaves, but walking was not too difficult on the even leaf mold. Barber peered here and there for denizens of the place to guide him. There were none, no more sound nor motion about than there had been in the park beyond Oberon's palace. The place was in a kind of silent green golden age as though the trees themselves had absorbed all the personality of the landscape. He struggled with the thought that they might similarly absorb him, turning his body into one of those rugose pillars, his members into branches . . . It was as credible as anything else in this land of unreason.

He was trying to follow a straight line by sighting on trees before and behind him, but could not be sure against following a wide circle.

Something moved.

In his familiar old world it would be an animal and perhaps dangerous. Still, Titania's wand ought to defend him against wug-wugs, whether predacious or fawning. He was acquiring respect for that ivory stick since the incident of the cloudless rain. He took a long, leaping step forward. The figure moved again, and now he was sure of its humanity.

"Hey!" he called.

The figure stopped; an old woman, leaning on a stick gripped in skinny hands, her long nose and chin curving toward each other like those of a caricature. Only these were visible under a floppy hat, and her head was bent to stare at the ground.

Barber bowed. "Beg pardon, ma'am, but could you tell me the way to the Kobold Hills?"

The head did not lift. " 'Tis bad loock to sleep near a apple tree. And beware o' t' ploom," said a voice that was so like Mrs. Gurton's as to make him start.

"Thank you," he said, "but can you tell me how to get to—"

" 'Tis bad loock to sleep near t' apple. And watch aht foor t' ploom." She showed him a shoulder and toddled off among the dark trunks.

Barber hesitated. If she didn't want to tell him, he had no means of compulsion, unless the wand. . . . But at least she was going somewhere, not round and round as he feared he himself was. He whirled and started after, but she had moved with surprising speed and was now no more than a flicker of motion far down the glades, held for a moment in a moonbeam, then gone completely.

No use. He groped his way back to the space where he had met the hag—or thought perhaps he had found it. Surely that oak whose boles had twisted themselves into a face that might belong to a villainous bishop was one he had seen before. Damn! Why couldn't Oberon have been more precise in his instructions? Doubtless imprecision as such was an element of this form of existence—if this were a form of existence and not the product of his own brain—an element as definite as vitamins in the world he knew. But if that were the case, Oberon certainly should not expect him to go to a precise place, the Kobold Hills, and perform a delineated action. The thought occurred to Barber that, if he acted on Fairyland precedent, he would probably be performing his mission by helping Jib write a commentary. It caused him to smile till a twig snapped somewhere in the moon-blue gloom and fear ran up and down his spine on little cold feet.

Something there, moving with him, parallel. No, it was not just the twig, he told himself, realizing that the small sound had been closer than the presence he suspected. The snap had called his attention to that presence, roused him from his own unawareness. It was there. Perhaps imagination? No, an almost imperceptible rustling, moving when he moved, stopping with him. No—imagination; nothing could synchronize its movements so exquisitely to his own. No, not imagination; that co-ordination could be achieved in this mad Fairyland where the physical laws in which he had been brought up didn't hold water.

"—didn't hold water," he caught himself saying the words aloud. This would never do, he was letting it get him. Ahead there was a little cleared space, with moonbeams slanting down across it. He raced for it, reached the edge, and stood gasping for his equilibrium; then jumped a foot, as a figure moved at the far

side. It was clad in flowing garments and took a step toward him. He clutched the wand in both hands, like a bat.

"Why, you're frightened!" trilled a soprano voice that ended in two notes of a laugh. "Don't fear me, mortal. I heard you in *the* forest, far away, and came to help you. Are you lost?"

Barber's muscles relaxed and he let the stick down as she came toward him, her face shadowed by a chaplet of leaves. "Yes, I am," he confessed. "I'm trying to get to the Kobold Hills. Perhaps you can help me find the way?"

Again the lilt of laughter. "But surely! Ah, none without the pure fairy blood can find their way without help through *the* forest. Come."

She had reached his side and taken his hand in her own, small and cool. The fear-feet were dancing on his spine still, but light as thistledown; there was something thrilling and pleasant in the frank contact of her hand, she led the way under the dark trees so straight and sure. He had stumbled across a root and came against her with shoulder and hip.

"Sorry," said Barber.

Her head turned and in the dark he thought she was smiling at him. "It's all right—how could you know the footways as I do? . . . You're very strong."

"I never thought so," said Barber practically, and then as this seemed an ungracious response to a conversational lead, added: "It's awfully good of you to—take charge of me like this."

"Not so. We of *the* forest are often lonely. To feel the pressure of a friendly hand is—sweet." Her fingers gripped his tighter for an infinitesimal part of a second.

She must have a cat's eyes for dark places, she was hurrying him along so fast. He wanted to go on talking to her, explore further this mysterious and rather attractive personage, about whom hung a faint sweet perfume of—what was it? . . . At least, he assured himself with a sudden return to the caution acquired by several years of social duties in the service, he wanted to get her into a light bright enough to make sure she didn't have buckteeth or piano legs. Even sausage makers' daughters from Milwaukee with halitosis and letters of introduction seemed to feel it a duty to turn the glamour on a diplomatic employee when they could get him alone under the fine moon of Europe. He remembered—

His guide suddenly swung him round a big tree with a crack-the-whip effect and stood facing him.

"Oh," she said, "here is the very door of my place. Will you not stay and rest for a few moments?" And as Barber groped for a formula of reluctance that would allow him to change his mind and accept with the least urging, she added: "If not for your own sake, at least for mine. I'm suddenly so tired."

An alarm bell rang in his head. That was a lie. She was not in the least tired. But Fred Barber was utterly lost now in this immense wood, and if she was lying to him, it was also likely that she had taken him far from his direction. He could only string along and find out.

"Why, I don't know—" he said, "I really must be making progress."

"Ah, I understand." Her head lowered and she let his hand fall. "I'm but a poor woods thing, and you used to great courts . . ." The fluting voice trailed off with an accent of the edge of tears.

"Oh, no; I was just going to say that I must be making progress, but I've already made about enough for tonight, so I can stop for a few minutes."

She took his hand again and led for half a dozen steps. A deeper black that would be a bank loomed out of the dimness ahead; his guide stooped and pulled aside a curtain of leaves. Warm fingers of yellow light reached from a short tunnel at whose far end Barber could see a room. He ducked through the door and followed her. At the far end she turned, laughing, and took both his hands in hers.

Neither buckteeth nor piano legs, but a good if somewhat well-developed figure, clad in a sheer dress splotched batik-wise in red, yellow, green, with a massive jeweled belt clasped round the waist. A blond head, cheeks cosmetic-red, though he could swear not from cosmetics, and eyes of a pronounced and startling green. Nice features, full lips; Barber smiled approval.

Her eyes widened in response, a little smile played across her lips as she drew his hands round till they met at her back. Her fingers slid up his biceps till they reached his shoulders, where they clung with a tingling pressure and her head tipped back. . . . "We in the wood are so lonely—so lonely," she sighed into his lips after the first contact. "Oh . . . you're strong. I didn't know a mortal could be so strong." Her eyelids fluttered against his throat; the perfume of her hair was intoxicating.

Was there something a trifle too rapid in this approach? The girl sighed and pulled his head down to meet her lips again. "Loose my girdle," she whispered.

His fingers fumbled with the clasp, and he undid it with pounding pulses. She slid from his arms a moment and tossed the belt clanking into the corner.

Fred Barber said: "I really ought to know your name."

She put up her arms again: "I have no name, my love."

The alarm bell rang again, loud and clear this time. She was lying. But why? And what did it matter, with this fascinating vision pirouetting slowly between him and the light? Barber remembered that there had been occasions when he threw a shoe at the alarm clock. Unfortunately, he also remembered there were usually consequences when he did it, and briefly cursed a temperament that could not take the moment without question as she slid into his arms again.

"No, really, what do people call you?"

"You may call me Malacea. Ah, love—"

Another bell jangled with a different timbre, far back in memory. The name ought to mean something, he could not think what. He talked desperately between long kisses. "How do you live? I mean, do you stay here always?"

"You will see. You'll stay with me. . . . We can be so happy, we two alone."

She's lying.

"Are you all by yourself?"

"Until you came." *That's a lie.* "But now we'll be together—forever." *That's another.* She tilted her head back. Again it came between him and the light, a curious light that flowed without visible source from a little bowl of bark, and Barber noted with a nervous shock that his hostess was ever so slightly transparent. There was something wrong—very wrong. He pulled away suddenly and sat down on the bed, which was of moss and let him sink into it. Think fast, Barber!

"Listen sweetheart," he said, reaching for her hand and holding it tight, "let's do this right. They warned me that all sorts of terrible things would happen to me if I didn't hurry up this mission I'm on, and I believe them. Can't you come with me as far as the Kobold Hills? It won't take long, and then we can both come back here . . . I like your woods."

Her eyes twitched and around her mouth little lines sprang into being that left her expression not half so attractive. "Oh, stay," she said, with a throaty sob in her voice. But Barber noted that the fingers of her other hand, resting against the wooden door pillar, were tap-tapping an irregular telegraphic beat, and her head cocked as though to hear an expected sound.

"How can I? You wouldn't want me to—turn into a frog in your arms?"

Tap-tap . . . and then, a duller sound, something approaching the cave with slow, heavy tread.

Malacea wrenched her hand free, snatched up Barber's wand, and raced down the tunnel.

He sprang to his feet and after, plunging through the leaf curtain with a rustle. For a moment he hung there, utterly blinded by a change from lighted room to tree shadow where only a few drops of moonlight filtered through, and out of that dark came the girl's voice:

"No—no. Please! You have the wand—that's all you need—ooh!"

The girl, just visible ahead of him, stumbled and fell as though strongly pushed. Between them moved a shadow, whose opposite side was outlined by a shaft of moon to the likeness of a leafless branch, shaped like a huge, gnarled hand. It was coming toward him.

Barber ducked, dodged behind a tree and looked up. Above him towered a figure, human in form, barklike in texture, twice his own size, semitransparent where it got between him and the moon. Its eyes held a dead fire of hate and cruelty, and the scraggy arms were reaching for him.

He turned and ran as he had never run in his life, dodging like a deer among the moon-splotched trunks. A root tripped him; he took three sprawling steps, recovered and went on; almost lost his footing over a small depression. Behind him, getting no nearer but certainly not receding, he heard the swish and crackle of the ogre's pursuit.

He slipped round one tree and was caught across the head by a low-hung branch, hard enough to bring a blinding flash across his vision. He kept on, feeling rather than seeing his way till sight cleared.

Another staggering trip must have cost him yards of

the small lead he held over the monster, and a trick of position threw the shadow of that clutching hand across a broad slash of moonlight before him. He could feel the wing-stumps quiver with instinct on his back; useless—and his second wind was going.

Racing on, he risked a sidelong glance. One of the huge hands was almost abreast, its fingers spread. Before him the forest suddenly opened into brilliant light and there was a stream, with flashing rapids right and left. A dark pool loomed before. Fred Barber put his last ounce of strength into a soaring broad jump.

He lost a shoe at the water's edge, and fell forward. In a last burst of vitality, he heaved himself to a knee and groped for something with which to defend himself.

The ogre towered from the other bank, looking down with those lidless eyes, its mouth working. It was partly transparent; the flooding moonlight on the thing cast only the thinnest of shadows through its shapeless carcass. For a few ticks of the watch, man and spook stared at each other across the rippling water. One of Barber's hands found the stone he sought.

The ogre turned and moved off among the trees, thump-thump on the leaf mold. If His Transparency wanted to call the matter quits, Fred Barber was certainly in no mood to pursue the matter further. It was not till the monster had disappeared from sight and sound that he remembered Oberon's words—"brooks . . . plagued ungainly obstacles to us of the pure blood, who must seek round by their sources or fly high above." That was why the pursuit had been given up. Or perhaps it had not; perhaps the ogre was on his way now to circle the stream at its headwaters.

Barber staggered dizzily forward. His forehead was growing an imposing bump and ached dreadfully.

He had not taken more than a dozen steps when

the pinwheels before his eyes ran together and he collapsed into a faint. The last thing he remembered before going out was Malacea's perfume. It was apple blossoms.

CHAPTER VII

Exhausted nerves and muscles must have turned his faint into normal sleep. He came to himself on his back, staring straight up. The incredible moon was already losing some of its light to a paling sky. He felt hungry, sore and abused. The ground, oozy-damp beneath, had left a trail of discomfort along his spine, and his head ached vilely, but he felt better.

The fact was, Barber told himself, lying there staring at the intaglioed surface of the earth's sister-star, and not caring to move lest it make the headache twinges worse—the fact was that being hunted through the woods by a translucent ogre out of a nightmare was a useful experience. It restored one's confidence in the reality of objective existence. Also in the ability of the corporeal senses to bear true witness of that existence, however their testimony might disaccord with preconceived notions of what it ought to be. His experience held no precedent for that wild chase through the forest, but lack of precedent was no reason for rejecting the memory—or his thoroughly physical bruises—as spurious. There had been no precedent for his first seasickness, either, but he had escaped from that when the ship reached dock. There didn't seem to be any docks on the shores of the sea of incertitude on which he was now launched.

No, it was real enough, and he did not doubt that if the ogre's woody fingers had closed about him they would have been real enough, too. So was the pressure of Malacea's breasts, round against him as he kissed her, though she was semitransparent. Well, the forest hag warned him against the apple—though how could he have known? The little bitch! . . . The thing to do was to learn the rationale of this system of existence into which he had somehow been projected, as one learned the new diplomatic code or the proper form of address for a first First Equerry. He—

At this point his meditations were interrupted by the unmistakable voice of the little bitch, her accent low and urgent:

"Let him wake. Oh, let him wake before the dawn."

Barber sat up and reached for the ache spot on his head. Malacea was facing him across the stream. She leaped to her feet: "Oh, my mortal lover!" she cried. "Come back; I know a spell to cure your pain."

"Yeah?" said Barber with hostility. "I know how you'd do it, too—turn me over to that Dracula boy friend of yours and have him fix me up so I wouldn't have to worry about any pains any more."

The light, whether of moon or coming day, was bright enough to show two big tears coming out on her cheek. "Ah, never, I swear it. My heart rose when you escaped the clutches of that demon Plum."

"That demon *what?*"

"Plum. I dare not but do as he asks. All the plums are hard and evil, but this one worst. His heart has dried and he wants a mortal blood transfusion."

"And you help him get it. Is that the idea?" Barber's voice was implacable.

"Oh . . ." Her fingers twisted against each other. "How can I make myself clean before you? How could I know that among the mortals that come to this wood would be my own dear love? Oh, come back, and help me repent; I'll make it good to you."

Barber, hunting among the long grasses for his dropped shoe, cocked an inward ear toward the alarm bell of his instinct for lies. Not a tinkle. She really meant it; or perhaps that new sixth sense merely did not work on emotional matters. "Thanks," he said, "but I'll stay over here out of reach of your friend. What happened to my wand?"

"You need not fear him. Listen, I'll prove my faith by giving you his secret. Wait for the sun; when daylight's abroad he cannot stir from his tree. You have only to eat of his fruit, then he can never harm you after. A hundred and fifty paces upstream will bring you to where the tree can be seen; it has a broken top."

"Unh." Barber found the shoe and put it on. It was wet. "Good. I'll wait till daylight and then try it."

"But come to me now. Oh hurry!" She looked up at the sky, now fully rose-colored along the horizon. "It's growing daybreak and I must go back to my own tree."

"What became of my wand?" repeated Barber.

"I don't know."

"You're lying."

She was weeping openly now. Barber, who had seen enough of both night-club life and diplomacy to develop some cynicism about feminine tears, flicked dried mud off his clothes without looking at her. Malacea stamped her foot: "The plum took it; where, I do not know. So you have my full confession; won't you—"

"No, I won't," said Barber. It seemed to him that his new sense of truth or no-truth was confused. Possibly Malacea suspected but did not definitely know where the wand was. He found a fallen trunk, tested it for solidity, and sitting down, opened the provision bag. Everything all right there, so far. Between bites, he said: "If you really want to impress me, you might tell me how to get to the Kobold Hills."

"Go straight on. Beyond the wood, you will reach a plain; walk through it for an hour or two, and when you see the hills blue on the horizon, you are near. But there be devils and strange things in that plain; I can see to guide you only so far."

Barber frowned, but there was no indication of any-thing but truth in her words. Watching him narrowly from beyond the stream, she suddenly became all gaiety.

"Oh, you'll return; I see it now. I am your fate and you mine. We are all, all avatars, though you are mortal and I only a tree sprite who can be seen through when the light is strong. Farewell then, for a little time."

"Good-by." He was beginning to relent a little; after all, she had been decent as far as she knew how.

"No, not good-by. We'll meet again and strangely." The tinkling laugh that had accompanied her first words when they met ran three notes up a scale and two down. "And you, mortal, will live weirdly before you lose yourself in finding yourself."

She took three steps among the crowding trees and was hidden, but behind her for a moment there floated the words of a song:

> "... fairies turn to men;
> When he touches the three—"

It was cut off abruptly and the wood went utterly silent as the first level ray of sunlight struck across the rapids in the stream.

Barber, dawdling over the remains of his breakfast, reflected that the downright approach of this child of nature was perhaps more appropriate to certain phases of international relations than to personal ones. There was something peculiar about the personal relations of Fairyland anyway, now that he came to think of it. The winged girl in Oberon's palace and, now, this one had practically thrown themselves at him. He could not honestly flatter himself into believing it was be-cause of any innate attractiveness of his own. Of course, his mortal appearance might be attractive to fairy girls . . . No—the Queen's attendant had described him as preternaturally ugly, if he remembered right.

There was also Jib and Cyril, both busy, who had been willing enough to drop their concerns and help him when he asked in the right way. It was as though Fairyland psychological reaction worked like a slot machine; you dropped in a penny, and unless it was counterfeit, got a stick of gum. No, not quite. There seemed to be some choice of reaction. He remembered Titania catching herself midway in a reply to one of Oberon's taunts, and the latter's abrupt shift to meet her mood—Malacea's lightning change from tears to happiness. It was more like a game of chess; you played pawn to king four on the board of personal relations and your opposite number, though not compelled to imitate you exactly, had to make one of a series of standard moves or find himself compromised.

If this held true as a general rule—Hold the boat, Malacea had just offered him a chance to give check to the king. Eat some of the dryhearted plum's fruit, and then be damned to him. He would need any such protections he could get after having lost Titania's wand, for he did not in the least doubt that queenly lady's word about his coming to "misadventured piteous overthrow" as a result. Action!

The plum tree was there, all right, standing pretty much by itself, as though none of the neighboring foliage cared to approach the monster. It was a very seedy old tree indeed, with pink blotches of fungus on its straggling leaves.

Barber waded the stream and approached it cautiously, ready to bolt. It took some inspection to reveal any fruit at all on it, but he finally located a couple—flat, wrinkly things, but plums. There was no sign of the wand. He wondered if the plum were hollow and the wand inside. It would be interesting to investigate; for that matter, it would be interesting to chop down the tree itself. That ought to settle Mr. Plum-spook's hash. But he had no ax, not even a knife; no matches to experiment with burning the thing down, and was not enough of a Boy Scout to start a fire by rubbing sticks.

The plums were well out of reach. A cast among the other trees gave him a dead branch, but it was not long enough. Two or three efforts to cast it javelin-wise gave no result.

Barber dropped the branch, wiped his hands, gripped the trunk of the plum and started to climb. The bark seemed to crawl beneath his hands—imagination probably. About him the malformed leaves rustled and the big old trunk heaved ever so slightly, as though in the grip of a stormwind. It creaked till he wondered whether it would break beneath him.

The branch with the fruit was one of the uppermost, and when he reached it Barber was driven to the uncomfortable expedient of swinging out along it, hand after hand, with his toes just balancing him on a lighter branch beneath. Under his weight the upper branch curved till he had difficulty keeping his grip, but the distance to the ground was not so great that he need fear a fall, so he kept on. Toward the end, he let go with one hand and grabbed. The fruit floated irritatingly away from his fingers, but at the fourth snatch he made it and tucked the plum in his jacket. Another effort gave him a second, and he dropped to the ground.

Close up, the plum looked even more unappetizing than from a distance, and a tentative nibble assured him that it tasted even worse—like a sour dried prune. No two ways about it, though; when you have to—

Cr-rrack! He looked up just in time to catch a glimpse of a big dead branch, unaccountably broken loose from the tree's morbid top, hurtling down at him. He jumped like a grasshopper, and sought the shelter of a friendly looking oak to finish his unpleasant snack. As he ate, he noted that the back of his jacket seemed tighter. Perhaps the wings were growing; but if so they were no use to him yet, so he set out to trudge his way along the banks of the stream.

The forest was very quiet in the dawnlight, almost as quiet as the strange parkland through which he had passed before, and he moved on without incident for a couple of hours till the trees on the left bank began to thin. Among their trunks he could see a line of yellow-brown where they stopped altogether, so crossed and made toward it. But when he got nearer he perceived that what he had taken for the packed earth of a sun-splashed plain was in fact a low, brown wall of some kind of adobe. It enclosed a space considerable both in length and in width, and entirely filled with rank on rank of gravestones, all alike in size except one very large one which faced a kind of gate a hundred yards from them.

Barber found the sight surprising; he had always supposed the inhabitants of Fairyland to be immortal, or nearly so. The wall was only about knee-high. He hopped over it and went to investigate this curious cemetery, in which the ground was not humped as it would be over real graves. The stones were very old; all the inscriptions had been weathered from them except a letter here and there. To make matters worse, the first two he examined had been lettered in Greek, a language with which he had had no contact since college days. From the next the lettering had disappeared entirely; there was only just visible the incised outline of a violin and a pair of musical notes. The next bore a book open, with the letters VERI, a gap, and AS. Then came one that had a crude representation of a telescope, another with faded armorial bearings, and one with the academic mortarboard cap. All had some symbol, and as Barber wandered among them he was struck by the fact that none of these symbols could by any imagination be considered either military or religious in character.

He made his way toward the larger and more elaborate stone at the gate. Like the rest it had been nearly effaced; unlike them it still bore a few traces of lettering beneath a coat of arms now nearly wiped out. Peering close Barber was able to make out in the crumbling stone:

> *"When the redbeard comes again*
> *Then shall . . . urn . . .*
> *When he . . . lac . . .*
> *He sh . . . faces."*

The illegibility of it was made still greater by the fact that it had originally been carved in old letter like the type face of a German book. Barber puzzled over it for awhile, but could make nothing of it, nor did there seem to be any other sign of life but a couple of lizards sunning themselves on the enclosure wall, so he left the graveyard and continued his way.

Beyond, the trees really were thinning out along the left bank of the stream. "Go straight on," Malacea had said, which he took to mean on along the river. It divided and flung one brooklike branch back among the trees, so he kept to the other. Along this fork the country was flat and soon became dismally bare, with the trees petering out into gray-green shrubs that had a greasy look under the now-high sun. Once or twice Barber caught a glimpse of something moving on the horizon, but too far and indistinctly for any details to be made out. The stream dropped away from him, down to the bottom of a stony arroyo, where it finally disappeared altogether.

It was hot. Barber called upon his foodbag for flasks of water, not without some trepidation, for in this region of no shade it had been impossible to keep the sun away from it. His respect for the frenetic little King's ability rose as the bag unfailingly answered his desires, but when he tried the container for cold bottled beer he got only a bitter liquid that made him quickly return to water.

But he was making progress. Looking back, he could make out a dark line of green rimming the horizon—*the* forest. In spite of his hard night, he felt strong and full of energy.

He plodded resolutely on. The dust-green shrubs had now mostly gone, the ground was all sand and pebbles with bunches of coarse grass here and there, across which he steered by the sun. The loneliness and silence of the landscape were beginning to weigh on him. Even the presence of the too-affectionate apple sprite would have been a relief, he decided, and began to wonder unhappily about what happened to people lost in deserts. They went cuckoo, didn't they? He couldn't remember, but to keep his mind off the empty landscape, he composed an imaginary report to the Foreign Relations Committee on conditions in England. It was not much help; he had written that report too many times before.

He tried composing scurrilous limericks on the Lords of Britain and imagined himself reciting them in Parliament. But this device also broke down on the failure to find a rhyme for "Norfolk," for it would never do to forget the premier Duke of the British Empire.

Miles of nothing.

Suppose he had been misdirected or had lost his way? Suppose he were isolated for keeps in this ironing board of a landscape? Oberon's bag would keep him in food and water, perhaps indefinitely, perhaps only to the next shaping, while he walked, walked, walked. Forever was a long time.

His beard would grow long and . . . whoa, there was a possibility of escape. His wings, those absurd shoulder-blade bunches, would grow too. He craned his neck around to look over his shoulder. There was certainly some kind of projection present, swelling his jacket to hunchback proportions. He tried using the new muscles at his chest, and could just see the projections wiggle. Interesting. He wondered if, when the wings came out, the ability to use them would grow too, or whether he would have to be pushed off a high place to learn how, like an eaglet from its nest. Who would catch him if he fell?

Consideration of the question diverted him till he noticed that his shadow had lengthened across the featureless plain and the sun was setting. Evidently he was to be caught out there for the night. Malacea had said it was only a walk of an hour or two—something wrong somewhere. He hoped it was only that she was a tree sprite and could not know this desert, but all the same the fear of this eternal emptiness came back and sat at the edge of his mind, waiting to be invited into the center.

There was no help for it at this moment. For better or worse he was stuck for the night. He sat down where he was, waited till the red ball of fire dipped under the horizon and then fished in the foodbag. Unlike the forest night, this one was brilliant with stars, though Barber, looking aloft, could recognize none of the constellations.

Stars. He and Kaja had picnicked under stars like that once. In sentimental memory, and to have something to do, he imagined her sharing the meal with him, and set aside the better half for her. But she was not really there, his conversational sallies remained unanswered, so Barber ended by eating both halves of the meal himself. Since there was nothing else to do, he scratched hip and shoulder holes in the sand and went to sleep.

The sun woke him by hitting him squarely in the eye. He stood up, stiff from his comfortless bed, and looked around. There was a line of hills, rimming the distance in plain sight, and they could only be the Kobold Hills, his goal at last. He emitted a shout of

delight which was lost in the immense silence, and
requisitioning a flask of water from the bag, started
briskly toward the hills.

But after an hour's walk they were dismayingly
smaller and more distant than before. It might, of
course, be optical illusion. He had heard of such
things in desert countries, though his personal experience extended no farther than the plateau of central Spain, where there was always a church or a house
or a sleepy muleteer to serve as a point of reference.
But it might equally be something connected with the
peculiar physics or geography of this realm. He looked
near and then far beside him, searching for some
feature by which he could orient himself.

The result was disconcerting. The desert close by
his side moved back as he strode along, as any well-
behaved desert should. But that in the distance crawled
slowly forward past him, faster than he. It was as
though the narrow strip on which he walked were an
endless belt conveyor, moving back faster than he went
forward. The optical effect was the familiar one he
had experienced as a boy, when he had looked for a
long time from a train window. When the train
stopped at a station the whole landscape would seem
to crawl for a moment in a direction opposite to its
previous motion. Only this time it really was moving.

He sat down discouragedly and flapped his wing-
stubs in annoyance. No result. He tried thinking his
way through the problem, but that did not get him
any forwarder.

As he did so, a movement caught his eye in the
direction of the hills. A little accumulation of blue-
black clouds was piling and tossing over there, their
summits glorious where the sunlight turned them
golden. There would be wind from the front of that
storm, thought Barber, and looked down toward the
desert in front of him. Sure enough four—a dozen—
twenty—any number of little dust clouds were jigging

and whirling across the desert toward him, and his
eye gladly followed this movement in the waste.

> *"It's up and over the Tongue of Jagai, as blown
>   dust devils go,*
> *The dun he fled like a stag of ten, but the mare
>   like a barren doe. . . ."*

Barber quoted to himself.

One of the whirlwinds was riding past within ten
feet of him. Suddenly its progress halted, and as
though that braking had converted all its energy into
angular velocity, spun more and more violently, denser
and denser, till it collapsed into a dirt-colored mannikin, not over two feet high, its head covered with
wobbly spikes.

"Hey, there, doc!" it shouted, bouncing and fidget-
ing in front of Barber. "Hey, there, Si! How's about
some gutbucket, huh? Um-pum, um-pum." It balanced adroitly on one toe, whirled till it was a blur,
and went round and round him.

"Beg pardon," said Barber, "but could you tell me
how to get to those hills?"

The thing stopped whirling and did handsprings
instead. "Aw, what d'you want to waste your time
there for, Mac? Only saps work. Come on down to
the clambake. We got a new scat-singer; you won't
have to watch no flutes swish. Diddy-boom, diddy-
boom. We'll make you a side-man—"

"Sorry, but I have to get to those hills. Business—
for the King."

"Oh, a Joe Union, eh? Thought you was a go-man."
The thing went into a wild calisthenic dance that
made it into a mere whirl of dust again, but the voice
came out of it. "What was it you wanted to get
smarted up on? *Hot*cha, *hot*cha."

"How to get to those hills. The more I walk toward
them the farther away they get."

"Chill it, handsome, chill it. Face away, look back over your shoulder, ankle backward toward 'em, and you'll be right in the groove." It danced on its hands. "What d'you play—Jibbo? Slushpump? Doghouse? Woodpile?"

"I'm not a musician, if that's what you mean." Barber stood up; the wind from the mountains was slightly chill about him, and the onrushing clouds were heaving huge shadows across the desert ahead.

"Not even a longhair? You mean you got *brains?*" It stood clapping, but trembling slightly in the wind. "Come on, be a satchel, be an alligator. Buddlydoop, buddlydoop."

The storm was coming on fast now, and Barber thought he could make out lines of rain beneath the clouds. All round and past him more of the dust whirlwinds were dancing, revealing now an arm, now a leg or a curious face. But they didn't seem to be getting away from the storm. "You wouldn't care to come with me, would you?" asked Barber.

"Who, me? Not when there's greasepots can sling a potful. I'm a rug-cutter; come on, gang, bite your nails." A dozen other individuals joined it in a spinning maze of acrobatics.

"But wait," said Barber, "won't that storm—"

"Aw, go get a permit!" The dust devils whirled around him, singing:

> *"What do we want with books of knowledge?*
> *Spin, you hep-cats, spin;*
> *You don't learn to spin in college;*
> *Spin the livelong day . . ."*

When that gets here we'll all have whiskers." With a shout of derisive laughter they were off. The storm was still rushing on, but now the hills stood out, black against its underedge. Barber tried walking toward them by the dust devil's method, backward, with his head over his shoulder. It gave him a frightful crick in the neck, but he found that by walking a hundred paces while watching over one shoulder and then changing to the other, he could ease the difficulty.

The storm, after all, proved one of those summer thundershowers, with a terrifying play of lightning along its front, a wind that tore briefly at him before it passed, and only a few big, wet drops. But as he changed from one shoulder to another to watch the nearing hills, he could see how it had swept away all the dust devils right before it, or beaten them out of existence. However, there would doubtless be more, and they were not very human anyway.

CHAPTER VIII

Dust devils were not the only things to think about.

Long before the hills were high about him, Barber was conscious of their clamor on that still air. The rhythm was set by an insistent metallic beat, up and down the scale like a set of tuned tympani, so near waltz time that he found himself thinking "The Blue Danube" to it. But as the sounds drew nearer and louder a melody joined the resonance; a chorus of many male voices from tenor to bass, singing indistinguishable words. The air was now gay, now melancholy, but always in the same fascinating three-quarter beat; for a bar or two Barber would catch the hint of something familiar in it.

Around him the ground was soaring into steeps and declivities; the soapy green shrubs of the desert had given place to scrub oak, birch and pines, then full-standing trees, their arms black-green in the westering light. Definitely among the hills now, he turned to walk forward in a more normal fashion, and was relieved to find the landscape had ended its antics, but the ceaseless song and drumming now changed direction, coming from one side, then the other. As he opened out a thickly wooded draw a great burst of the music came charging down at him; among the trees in that direction were freshly cut stumps, and high up in the side of the hill a glare of warm red light challenged the dying sun among the branches.

An entrance of some kind—should he chance it? He

hesitated for a moment, then decided against. After all, he could return, there was not the vaguest hint of a plan in his mind. Even if he made one, whatever lay beyond the next spur would probably cause him to modify it. He pressed on, noting that along here the ground was seamed with little paths, crisscrossing among the trees, pale in the fading gloom. From a hill on the left another rollicking chorus swept at him, another beam of red light plashed across a fan of tailings at an entrance to the hills.

As he stood looking at it the thought came to him that one of the most striking things about Fairyland was its sameness. There was no escaping an experience; whatever one did, whichever way one turned, it was repeated until a solution had been found. Like the case of Three-eyes on the road here. Apparently whatever force controlled his destiny was driving him toward those cave entrances. Wondering whether he had solved the problem of Malacea satisfactorily, he turned toward the entrance and began to climb.

Just before his head came level with it a new note, high and piping, joined the roaring melody of the chorus. It was a bird song, a nightjar, perfect in time and melody, and Barber recognized the tune as that of the "Waldweben" from *Siegfried*.

Ominous. But no use turning back now. He drew a breath, heaved himself across the rubble heap and stepped into—

A short passage, with a smooth-polished stone floor, slanting slightly down into a great hall whose upper reaches were lost in smoky dimness. It was filled with tables and lined with guttering red torches in brackets. Every seat at all those tables was occupied by a little man, but there was no type resemblance—some clean-shaven with round, jolly, cherubic faces, some skinny with goatbeards, some with jowls and pointed mustaches. They had mugs of beer before them, and barmaids in bright dresses were hurrying among the tables with more. As Barber watched, a fat elf pinched one of the girls on the buttock. She jumped, tripped and came down with a crash; one of the dwarfs at the nearest table emptied his beer mug on her head, and as the dripping face came up, those near by burst into roars of laughter, clinging to each other's shoulders, helpless with merriment.

The incident passed unnoticed in the general uproar, for the singing Barber had heard during his approach was now clear as coming from the throats of these drinkers, who were pounding out the time with their mugs. But it was not quite the joyous concord he had heard from a distance. Every little group of kobolds and sometimes every kobold in a group was working away on a different song, flatting hideously. Whatever pretense to harmony the din could make was accidental, the result of one set of voices striking into the right note to accord with those of another lot six tables away. Only the metallic waltz beat of the drumming, louder now, lay under and united the clashing sounds.

Barber was granted time to observe so much before the kobolds at the nearest table noticed him. They stopped singing and stared at him with slack jaws, whispering and pointing, drawing more after them till silence spread across the room like ripples on a pool. It had nearly reached the far end, where the doors through which the barmaids came were barely visible, when three kobolds, neatly uniformed in gray, came hurrying toward him. The leader wore a badge in complicated gold filigree. He bowed low before Barber, and said:

"Good evening, highborn sir. It is my pleasure to extend you the welcome of the Kobold Caverns. How intelligent of you to come and see the wonders of our beautiful place with your own eyes! May I hope you will be with us for a long time? Will you permit me to join you in a glass of beer?"

The last words came out loud in an enormous silence punctuated only by the waltz drumming. Barber knew what it was now; it was the sound of
hammers.

"Why, I wouldn't mind some beer, thanks," he said.
"But what I really want is to see whoever's in charge
here. I'm an ambassador from King Oberon, and—"

A vertical frown leaped into being between the gray
dwarf's eyebrows. "Excuse, please," he said, and turning to the room, threw up his arm. "Go on!" he
shouted. "This does not concern you." All over the
room faces turned back to the tables and the uproar
of song instantly began again in full volume. Gold-
badge turned back to Barber.

"Ah," he sighed, "observe how cheerful the dear
fellows are. Only the industrious can be so truly
happy. Is that not the answer to the slanders that are
pronounced against us? Will you come this way,
please?"

He gripped Barber's arm and steered him down an
aisle between two tables of shouting kobolds, with the
other two guides coming along behind. "I trust you
enjoyed your journey, highborn sir?" He glanced at
Barber's shoulders, then sighed again. "Ah, but you
winged fairies are fortunate—born in a different world,
so to speak. All we poor kobolds obtain we must earn
by the sweat of our brows."

Barber thought of his trip through the desert and
smiled internally. "You seem to have made yourselves
very comfortable here, though," he said courteously.
It would not do to push matters about the swords.

"We do our best. All we ask is peace in which to
carry on our honest labors." He swung Barber around
at a table in a recess where five bearded kobolds were
trying to sing a part song but missing badly because
none of them seemed able to remember when he
should come in. "Here we are. You can go." He motioned to the occupants of the table. Two of them

stood up docilely enough, but the one at the back brought his beer mug down with a bang.

"This is organized inefficiency!" he bawled. "I'll make a report to the section! I'll—"

He came to a mouth-open stop as Barber's guide stepped forward, fingering the filigree badge, then leaped to his feet, bowing and knuckling his forehead. "I beg your humble pardon, worshipful sir. I did not know you were authorized. I—"

"Next time it will be the White Pit," said Gold-badge evenly. "Please be seated, highborn sir, and try our kobold beer. Drink—and die, you know; don't drink—and die anyway. Therefore, let's drink. Ha, ha, ha."

"Ha, ha, ha," clacked his two companions in obedient chorus. A mug of beer was thrust into Barber's hand. It was delicious, somewhat with the flavor of bock, but had a tang that gave warning of a particularly heady brew.

"Are you not partly of mortal kindred, highborn sir?" inquired Gold-badge. "I thought so; something about the eyes. You will enjoy seeing our mushroom plantations. Krey here can show you all through them. He used to be a deputy in the Provender Section."

"Till the medical discovered I had a natural affinity for beer," said one of the gray-clads. He had a young face and pleasant smile over a jaw heavy enough to be cast iron.

"I'd like very much to see them sometime," said Barber, "but just at present I'm here on really important business."

"Oh, business!" All three burst into a gale of laughter, which the two assistants ended by sputtering into their beer, while Gold-badge laid a hand on Barber's arm. "Pardon us, highborn, sir, but it is not permitted to discuss business at this hour in the Kobold Caverns."

That beer was heady; Barber could feel a spot of warmth on each cheekbone. But he was not so far gone as to miss the fact that this was a particularly elaborate version of the run-around. He grinned to show appreciation of a joke on himself, and pushed ahead: "You'll have to excuse me. I don't know your local customs. But I'm an ambassador and by international custom have the right of transacting business at any time."

"So?" Gold-badge's eyes narrowed a trifle. "I did not really understand, highborn sir. It is most fortunate that we have met; for in addition to being of the Incoming Section which receives guests, I am also of the Welcoming Section to greet ambassadors. Doubtless you have special credentials to prove your character—our lady Titania's wand, or His Radiance's ring, or even a mere warrant in writing?"

"I did have but I—" Shame flooded Barber at the memory of how he had lost the wand and he came to a halt. The triple laughter blended into the sound of the ceaseless waltz song, and Gold-badge dug him in the ribs:

"Ha, ha, ha! Never mind, *Mr.* Ambassador, we won't give you away. We take things easy in the Kobold Caverns and the drinks are on the government. Finish that one and have another."

Barber drank.

At one point in the subsequent proceedings he caught himself trying to explain the Binomial Theorem, of which he knew rather less than his audience, to a group that seemed passionately interested. At another he was leading them in a vigorous rendition of "The Bastard King of England." Then Gold-badge seemed somehow to have slipped away, the hall and chorus were gone, and he was descending a long, dim passage with Krey and the other gray-clad receptionist; a passage where the only sound was the three-quarter beat of the forges.

The passage slanted in involuted curves under a ceiling just tall enough to give him headroom. Torches smoked on the walls here and there, dripping an occasional spark, and where their light fell strongest the wall was perspiring in big, dank drops. The black mouths of other tunnelings yawned to right and left at each turn; there were no lights in them.

". . . our mountain mushrooms, cooked in a butter of beechnuts," Krey was saying, "I have *mush room* in my stomach for them. Ha, ha, ha."

"Ha, ha, hahaha," the passage echoed sepulchrally. At each branching tunnel the sound of the hammer-beats was louder and clearer. When they reached the next turn-and-entrance Barber pretended to stagger, and a little illogically vexed at finding how easy it was to let himself go, clutched vainly at the smooth wall, slid and lay with his head half in the side tunnel. The hammer blows drowned Krey's footsteps (he had on some kind of soft shoes) but Barber's ear caught the accent of his voice and the note of a retreating laugh. Bumpity-bump, bump-bump, bump-bump went the hammers to the sound of a mentally hummed "Blue Danube"; and the floor was cold stone, but an enormous alcoholic weariness invaded Barber's limbs and it was suddenly pleasant to lie right there.

"Mus' get up," he told himself fuzzily, but only managed to twitch a leg while half his brain cried a warning to a too-well-satisfied other half.

Clang! Somebody dropped something. The eldritch idea assailed Barber that the sound represented the fall of Krey's face when that strong-chinned worthy discovered his disappearance. Laughter released his paralysis; chuckling over the inane drunken humor of the idea, he pulled himself to knees, then feet. The side passage was as black as the inside of a dog, sloping down rather steeply, and he had to keep one hand on the wall for support as well as direction. But fifty or a hundred yards on it turned suddenly and he found himself at the head of a flight of low steps, looking down into a wide cavern. There was a torch in the wall near him; it showed a shapeless mound of something occupying the whole center of the cave, covered over with a cloth. Right at the head of the stairs was a small iron bar set across the passage about two feet up. The latter puzzled him till he remembered that the kobolds were the only people of Fairyland who could touch iron. The bar would be good as a locked door to anyone but himself, but he stepped over it and down the stairs.

The cloth was loose. He lifted one edge and gave a whistle, for there they were: rapiers, sabers, claymores, panzerstechers, yataghans, cutlasses, and dozens of other kinds of swords whose names he did not even know, each kind in its own bundle and thousands of them altogether. This was what the kobolds were trying to hide from him all right, but what could he—

"So."

The tone was even, but nasty. Barber, a cold perspiration of sudden sobriety making a little spot between his shoulder blades, turned and looked into the eyes of Krey. The pleasant smile was gone; in the second or two that they stood gazing at each other, the kobold fumbled a little silver whistle out of his tunic and blew. Instantly there were shouts and the sound of running feet; another door at the back of the room, which Barber had not noticed, was filled with dwarfish figures.

For a moment the idea of seizing up one of the blades and slashing out among them leaped through Barber's head—but where would he go among those complex tunnels? Krey seemed to follow his thoughts.

"I advise you not to attempt resistance," he said coldly. Barber noticed that among the crowding kobolds at the back door a disciplined battalion with spears in their hands were pushing forward. The heads of the spears were leaf-shaped and looked extremely sharp. He dropped his hands at his side in a gesture of surrender.

"It is too bad," Krey went on, "that you must spoil a fine evening by abusing the hospitality of the Caverns. Now you must bear the consequences . . . Take him to the trial room!"

One of the spearmen jabbed Barber in the leg. He jumped and yelped. "Damn it! I didn't ask for your hospitality and I don't think very much of it. I'm here as an ambassador and I claim diplomatic immunity."

"Diplomatic immunity confers no license to break the criminal laws." Krey turned his back; the guards closed round Barber, and with lowered spear points, shepherded him toward the back door of the room. There was a passage with torches; it branched, and Barber was urged down the fork to the right, along a ramp and through an arch.

He was in a long and high cavern from whose walls and ceiling projected elaborate carved wood dingleberries in the most atrocious taste. At the far end a kobold with a long nose and prick ears was seated before a table on a low dais, writing feverishly and surrounded by a perfect mountain of papers. The way to his seat was lined by a double row of kobold guards with swords in their hands, standing rigidly and staring at each other. Barber was urged down the alley between them to the foot of the dais, and one of the spearmen let the butt of his weapon drop to the floor with a thump.

The long-nosed kobold looked up with a sour expression. "Guard Section Eleven. Prisoner found spying in arsenal room. Authorization of Krey, Incoming Section Four," said the spearman, in the metallic voice of an old-fashioned phonograph.

"Look here," Barber burst in, "you're going to have some trouble about this. I'm a perfectly legal ambassador from King Oberon and—"

Long-nose took a new sheet of paper and scribbled. "Your protest is noted and rejected," he cut in. "All residents of the Kobold Caverns, whether metic or natural, are subject to the same restrictions. I sentence you to—"

"But I'm not a resident!" cried Barber desperately. He could see two of the sword-bearers start toward him, and the thought of what the sentence might be gave him cold shivers. "I'm not even a resident of Fairyland. I'm a mortal."

Long-nose's brows elevated. "A mortal! Just a moment, please, I must find a precedent. Though I warn you it will not be so pleasant for you, since you have now added perjury to the other charge. Mortals do not have wings." He turned to one of the mounds of papers which reached desk-high from the floor, and began shuffling through them. They had not been disturbed for a long time, apparently, for a little cloud of dust rose from them. Long-nose's face worked convulsively, his head went back, and he emitted a thundering sneeze.

"God bless you," said Barber automatically.

"Yeeeee!" All the kobolds together joined in the ear-piercing shriek. The spearmen dropped their spears, the swordsmen their swords, the long-nosed judge jumped over the table, and all together they raced for the exits. In two minutes Barber was left alone with the discarded weapons, the mound of papers and the gingerbread carving.

CHAPTER IX

Barber picked up a few of the swords. Oberon had certainly told him not to use force on the kobolds and it seemed that other methods were more effective—why hadn't he remembered from the beginning that medieval legend always mentioned the name of God as anathema to these people of the hills? Still, one of these swords would be a handy object if he encountered the Plum or other monsters of that ilk. Most of the weapons were too small, but he found a claymore which, being designed for both a kobold's little fists, was about right for one of his own.

Doorways led in several directions among the forest of lambrequins, and the way he had entered by was not promising. He chose an exit at random and found himself in one of the usual passages, which ran on, dipping and winding past rooms dark and rooms lighted. All were untenanted, and Barber was conscious of something vaguely wrong in the air, as impalpable as a thought. He tried to shake it off, tried to hum "Blue Danube"—and then it came to him what the difference was. The undertone of the hammers, no longer so loud, had changed from the three-four beat of a waltz to the four-four of march time.

The passage also had changed character. Its walls and ceilings were trued off smoothly now, no longer dripped, so that it was like a corridor in an office building. A few yards ahead the feeble light showed a pair of bronze doors with a complex design in massive relief. Barber put his ear to the doors. Not a sound within. He pushed one of them gently. As it swung back on hinges oiled to silence the design impressed him as so familiar that he bent to examine it. A coat of arms—where had he seen the like before, with its repeated crowns and eagles and singular half-a-bear? Of course; it was the design he had seen more than half-effaced, on the big tombstone in the graveyard at the edge of *the* forest, but here there was no lettering with it. But that was not all; some insistent memory nagged at him till he stopped and hunted it down, tried to localize it. That design ought not to be on a door—when he had seen it before, somewhere, it was *worn*. Barber gave up, shrugged his shoulders, and pushed in.

Beyond the door was another hall, huge as that of the drinkers, but only feebly lit by a couple of torches. Their flames reflected redly on bright stone of walls and floor; the ceiling was lost in gloom. Barber caught his breath sharply at the sight of what seemed to be human figures in niches all down the walls. Inspection showed them to be suits of kobold-size Gothic armor, with the visors of the armets down so that it was impossible to tell whether they held living creatures.

He stepped over to the nearest and touched it on the plastron with his sword. It gave forth a metallic scrape rather than the ring of hollowness, but remained immobile, and when he tried to lift the visor that mechanism would not budge.

Barber turned toward the far end of the hall. It held a long, low table, with a row of chairs down one side. At the end was a much larger chair, with a low seat but a high, intricately carved back and damask upholstery. It looked like a throne.

Barber walked the length of the hall to examine this throne more closely. There was nothing special about it, but set into the wall behind it was a copper plate with lettering on it. Barber bent to puzzle out the Gothic inscription:

> *"Of places three*
> *The one you see*
> *Fyrst touched shall bee."*

Meaningless. Or perhaps not quite. He remembered a line of Malacea's song:

> *"When he touches the three places—"*

Perhaps he was supposed to touch this one. Perhaps this was what Oberon meant by the enterprise he had been brought here for. Just for the hell of it, he reached out and touched the plate with the point of his sword.

Crash!

The room stood out vivid in a blue-white flash of lightning, then pitched into darkness while thunder rumbled to and fro among the caverns like ten thousand cannonballs rolling downstairs. Barber froze while the thunder died, straining his eyes against the black, more than half expecting, and certainly hoping, that the returning light would show the well-ordered interior of Gurton's cottage. Every hair follicle on his face tingled till his jaw seemed on fire, and he felt a sudden tug at the back of his jacket where the wing-cases were.

The room slowly returned to normal, the fiery pin-wheels before his eyes disappearing. He looked round. He could swear that the halberd in the hand of that suit of armor swayed. The torches were guttering out, darkness creeping from above like a spider lowering itself on its thread. He heard a faint, fricative sound, that might be breath whistling in and out through the holes of a visor, and realized with a shock that the hammer sounds in the distance had gone altogether dumb.

There was a faint scrape of metal on steel plate and then, small but startling in the silence, the sound of a cough. Barber turned and trotted on tiptoe down the length of that shiny expanse of stone. The end seemed twice as distant as before, like the vanishing point in a diagram showing the laws of perspective. Before he reached it he was frankly running. At the last moment torches gave a final flicker and went out together. He made the last few strides in darkness, located a door handle by feel and tugged it open, with a sense of wild relief.

No more than before did he have any idea where he was, and now all those passages were more than ever void, with not even the sound of the forges to keep him company. Neither was the pitch of the tunnels any help; they turned up and down after a fashion that had no logic. But the luck that had run with him through the caverns still held, and after an hour or more of wandering he reached a fork where one passage led to the drab pallor of daylight instead of the ubiquitous torch-glow.

The sun had just risen when he came to the mouth, up on a high hillside looking out across a rolling and grassy champaign, quite unlike the desert through which he had trekked to reach the place. Off in the middle distance, half hidden by the intervening rolls, was a group of brown and yellow rectangles that would be a farm or its Fairyland equivalent. Beyond, the darker green of trees.

There would be life of some sort there and not kobold life. Barber went down the hillside in long, leaping steps, his lungs glad of the fresh air.

It was like a late summer morning in New England with dewy spiderwebs on the grass and a few early midges in their aerial dance above. Grasshoppers sprang out from before his feet, whirred away over the rich meadow. Each rise brought the buildings nearer. At the fourth the group of buildings became definitely farm; from the next a horse was visible, pegged out in a field and cropping the lush grass, and from the next again he spotted a man working over a patch of bare earth.

Barber paused at the lip of the last rise and rubbed his fingers through a considerable growth of whisker. His appearance was certainly odd enough to cause alarm, but there was no razor handy, nor did he feel like dropping the sword, his only protection.

From the top of the hill he could see the farm spread before him in orderly checkerboards marked off by stone fences. The farmer did not look up till he heard the sound of a displaced stone as Barber climbed over the nearest fence. He was a big, burly man with rolled-up shirt sleeves and a pair of gaudily checked pants sustained by a single gallus at the top, and at the bottom tucked into jackboots. As Barber drew near, he turned a ruddy face in which a pair of startlingly blue eyes looked out over gray-flecked sideburns. His glance fell on the sword; without wasted motion he dropped his hoe, stepped lightly to an angle of the fence and picked up a formidable looking broadax. Feet spread, he stood facing Barber without hostility or fear.

"Hello," said Barber.

The farmer replied: "Howdy, mister." He relaxed a little and lowered the ax. "Nice mornin'."

"Yes, it is," agreed Barber judicially. "My name's Barber."

"Glad to make your 'quaintance, Mr. Barber. Mine's Fawcett, Noah Fawcett. Where you from?"

"King Oberon's place."

"Be you one of the heathen?"

"I'm not a fairy, if that's what you mean."

"Don't believe in fairies. They're just heathen. You work for Oberon?"

"Yes. I'm an ambassador."

"Well, I declare to goodness. Where was you from originally?"

Barber smiled. "Lansing, Michigan, if you want to go back that far."

Noah Fawcett frowned. "Don't guess I know—say, d'you mean Michigan Territory?"

"It's a state now. Admitted to the Union in 1835."

"Well, by the tarnal nation. Harry Clay allus said we ought to take her in. A real American." Fawcett dropped his ax definitely now and stepped forward to shake hands. "Come on in and make yourself t'hum, mister. How old be you? Be you married? What's your church? Be you Whig or one of those Damocrats? How'd you come to work for Oberon? What's the news from back in the States?"

Barber's movement of desperation halted the spate of inquiry and Noah Fawcett gave a deep, chesty laugh. "Guess I'be jumpin' ahead of the thills, but I ain't see ary man but the swandangled heathen for a right long spell, let alone a real American. Get pretty lonesome for news." He was leading the way to the larger of a pair of clapboarded buildings. Inside, there was not even paint on the neat plaster, but the room was cluttered with substantial-looking furniture dominated by a wooden pendulum-clock, which was ticking busily. Everything had the indescribable look of sophisticated design Barber had noted in articles made by Continental peasants.

Noah Fawcett caught his glance. "Yep," he said, "made the hull business, mostly winters when they wan't nathin' else on hand. 'Through the idleness of hands the house droppeth through,' the Good Book says. That rack, now"—he indicated a pair of jigsawed brackets against the wall—"was for a gun. But I never could get a barrel, even from the mountain heathen, and they're pretty cute about ironwork. You can put your sword there. That's a funny hump on your back. Was you hurt when you was little?"

"No. I guess it just grew there."

Fawcett shook his head. "Better be careful of that, Mr. Barber. I had a cousin over to Lou-isy had one of those lumps come on his chest, and the doctor said how he died of it. But I don't put much store by doctors. Now you set down and I shall get some wherewithal to celebrate. Be you married?"

Without waiting for Barber's reply he lifted a trap door and dived into a cellar, to return in a moment with a jug. "Berry wine," commented Fawcett, pouring some into a pair of wooden mugs with a pleasant glugging sound. " 'Taint's good as the cider I make, but I'm a little mite short-handed, and have to go a long piece for m'apples. How come you to work for the heathen king? Does he pay good wages? He's all right for a heathen, but they're all like Injuns and woodchucks; it won't do to take ary sass from them. Had a run-in with him myself a while back."

He chuckled at the memory. Barber experienced a sudden twinge of embarrassment at the thought of his own ready acceptance of the authority of the "heathen" court, and was glad he had not mentioned the incipient wings. "How did that happen?" he asked, to keep the conversation on safe lines.

"Passel of plaguey whoop-te-tiddle about some logs. When I come here I made a deal, fair and square, to farm this land and swap my produce. I built me that little sod house you seen outside. Come fall, I went down to the river to get stun, and found a hull batch of apple trees, so I grubbed up some of the littlest and planted 'em round my house. They growed all right, but I had to get rid of 'em." Fawcett paused dramatically to take a pinch of snuff, and held out the box to Barber, who declined and asked the expected: "Why?"

"The heathen. At night, they'd come dancin' around, wavin' their arms and scowlin' suthin' meta-phorical. They was dressed up in bark like they was tryin' to give me a chivaree. We Fawcetts don't scare easy. When I went out to give 'em a piece of my mind they all took after me. I pulled foot back into the house and grabbed my ax. Right there I larnt that must of the heathen is tarnal 'fraid of iron. Some superstition of theirn. Long as I had that ax they wouldn't come nigh me . . ." Fawcett bent to a boot-jack. "Pull off your shoes and be comfortable, mister."

Barber was willing enough to do so. The shoes given him by the King's tailor had been comfortable enough in the beginning, but the unwonted amount of walking he had done lately seemed to have spread his feet so much that they were tight; it was a relief to get rid of them. "I thought you said it was some-thing about logs," he said.

"I'be comin' to that. They kept comin' around at night. When I asked 'em why they couldn't let a Christian sleep, they told me they was sperrits of the trees. Now I'be a moderate man, but it says in hun-dred and first Psalms, 'He that telleth lies shall not tarry in my sight,' and furthermore, 'Regard not them that have familiar sperrits,' so that got my dander up. I cut down those trees and used the logs to start my little log house that's a corncrib now. Well, I like to had a heathen uprisin' on my hands."

He made another dramatic caesura, emphasized it by getting up to refill both mugs, and asked with elaborate offhandedness: "Have much trouble with uprisin's out in the new states?"

"Not very," Barber smiled. "But what happened? How did you put down the uprising?"

"Well, the heathen came round agin, yellin' no-toriously, and makin' out I'd massacreed a mort of their relations. They was goin' to tell the King and

have the law on me. 'Law ahead,' says I, knowin' I
had the King's leave to farm this land, and the guv'-
ment's word has to be better'n the next man's or he'd
be runnin' things. So I went down to the river and
got some more trees. I skided 'em out with Federalist—"

"Who?" interrupted Barber.

"Federalist. My hoss, that the King guv me when
we made the deal. I finished my house; but it just
goes to show what the Good Book says: 'Put not thy
trust in princes.' Along come that King, madder'n a
nest of hornets and wanted to cancel the hull deal
and put me off my land. I told him I was a citizen of
the U-nited States and protected by its constitution,
that says the obligations of contract shall not be im-
paired, the way John Marshall told 'em in that there
Georgia land case, a few years back. Well, he hemmed
and he hawed, and the heathen with him ripped
around till I got tired of hearin' 'em. I told him we
Bay Staters fit a war to get rid of one king, and if he
was minded to see how we did it, I'd show him right
there.

"That didn't take him so good; he fizzed like a firin'
pan, and I thought we was goin' to have real troubu-
lous times, till all of a sudden it come over me to
say: "See here, my hearty, there be more of us Fawcetts
comin' this way, so you better not try ary monkey-
shines with the first one. I'be a moderate man. If
those trees are special pets of yourn, you could tell me
so without a lot of cock-and-bull about sperrits, for
I'do not believe in vain boastin', as is related in the
first book of the Kings of Israel, twentieth chapter. 'I
shall make you a hoss trade,' I said to him. 'If your
people'll deliver me good sound timber for some of
my produce I shall leave your pet trees be.' By and
by he ca'med down and seen the sense of it, and that's
how it's been ever since. But it seems agin nater to

have a farm without a wood lot. I guess now I've done enough talkin'. Tell me about your trip here, mister. See ary Injuns? How'd you come by the sword?"

One sentence in the narrative had caught Barber's attention. "Oh, I got that from the—kobolds in the mountain," he parried. "But didn't you say something about more of you Fawcetts?"

The farmer sloshed the lees of his drink around the bottom of the mug and tossed it off. "Brothers," he answered briefly. "Obadiah and Lemuel—he married one of the Whiting gals. They was goin' to leave Middlesex County the summer arter me, and follow right along the Albany trail. But it's been a mighty long time, and I sometimes consider mebbe they got caught by the Injuns or some of those other heathen . . ." He glanced at the clock. "Time to put the victuals on," he said in a changed tone, and got up.

CHAPTER X

Just before sunrise Barber was wakened by a large hand on his shoulder. For a few sleepy moments he stared uncomprehendingly upward at the side-whiskered face and the wall beyond, his body savoring the comfort of bed after many nights on the ground.

"Time to lay into the chores, mister," said Fawcett cheerfully.

Barber stretched, yawned, and touched a prickly chin. The assumption that he had signed on as a farm hand struck him as pretty cool, but he contemplated the prospect without resentment. Perhaps Oberon had intended it that way. "Have you got an extra razor I could borrow?" he asked.

"Well, now that I think," replied the farmer, "that's one thing there be'nt in this hull place. They's a virtoo in the water or suthin' that makes a man's hair stay put; mine ain't growed a mite since I'been here." He looked at Barber, pulling on his clothes, with his face carefully turned to keep the incipient wings at his back out of sight, and laughed. "Don't know's I'blame you, though, with a brindle bush like that. Let's have suthin' to 'strengthen by the sperrit, the inner man' as the Apostle Paul wrote to the Ephesians. I consider I'be lucky, without ary stock to feed before I'can have my breakfast."

Barber's eye caught the foodbag, where he had hung it on the back of a chair the night before, and, "I think I can help you out there," he offered brightly. "Is there anything you'd specially like but haven't been able to get lately?"

Fawcett's whiskers moved in a grin. "Well, now you call it to mind, there is. I declare there's times when I would give 'most all I own for a chunk of good Boston codfish. Ain't got that, have you?"

"Watch me." Barber concentrated on the thought of codfish and reached into the bag. It yielded a handful of crumbling leaves and the musty odor of decayed vegetation. Slightly dismayed, but remembering how it had failed on beer during the journey, he tried again, but made the request plain ham and eggs. Same result. Fawcett was surveying the proceeding disappointedly.

"What under the canopy be you tryin' to do?" he demanded. "Bamboozle me?"

"It worked yesterday," Barber protested. "Probably the sun got at it. Oberon's chamberlain warned me it might go wrong if that happened. I'm sorry; I wasn't trying to fool you." He felt his face flushing; this was as bad as feeding horse meat to a Congressman.

The farmer emitted a snort and clumped heavily toward the stairs. "No call to take on," he said. "When you git to know the heathen 'swell as I do, you'll larn suthin' about those conjurin' tricks of theirn. They talk about them till you would think they could make the sun stand still, like Joshuar over Gibeon, but what's it amount to? 'Profane and vain babblin's' as the Good Book says in First Timothy. I call to mind the time I'planted some cukes in that little gusset of land down by the river. They come up measly little things with funny leaves. That upset the mountain heathen suthin' scandalous. They're almighty fond of cukes."

He was laying out the breakfast with slouching efficiency. "What happened?" Barber encouraged him.

"Why, they come to me, and they said: 'There has been a shapin' and your cukes have turned into ivy plants. But never you mind,' they said, 'we shall undertake to conjure 'em back for you.' I told 'em to go right ahead, long's they didn't step on the plants. Nathin' much tenderer'n a young cuke. Well, the hull kit-'n-boodle of 'em come down from the mountain and pow-wowed round half one night, and sure enough, the cukes growed all right arter that."

Fawcett seated himself at the table and began to eat, waving Barber to another chair. "Do you mean the conjuring really helped the cucumbers?" asked Barber.

The farmer chuckled through a mouthful of food. "Don't you think I'be in my right senses? It wan't the shapin' that like to spoiled the cukes or the conjurin' that saved 'em. Hoss manure is just no good for cukes; I knowed that when I'put 'em in, but it was all I had. But the day before the heathen did their fancy tricks I'found a salt lick back in the woods a piece and got some good deer manure that did the business. The heathen had the gall to ask for a reduction in the price of the crop. . . . Well, the way seasons run here, I guess mebbe we could get in a little buckwheat today."

Barber was city-bred, and had never before experienced the contentments that rise from watching and producing the growth of the soil—seeing bare earth sprout delicate green hairs one day, so fine they were almost invisible except as a sheen; three days later returning to find them tiny but palpable plants, and in a week sturdily putting forth leaf and branch. Their growth seemed so swift that everything else was slowed to a timeless wheel of night and morning through which he moved in occupations that varied only by the width of a finger from each other. His own world and his Embassy job seemed too far away and long ago to be of more than academic interest. For that matter so had the question of returning to them.

During the day he worked in the fields, sometimes

hoeing little mounds of earth around the stalks of the growing corn, sometimes picking early crops like peas and beans—for it was high summer and these were coming on ripe—and helping Fawcett arrange them in drying racks for preservation. He had tried to explain to the New Englander the better process of canning. But there were neither cans nor Mason jars with which to give a demonstration, and as always when he spoke of modern conveniences, Fawcett guffawed, treating the idea as one might the performance of an imaginative child. As early as the third day Barber had given up trying to tell him about such modernities as electric light and skyscrapers. The farmer received the informations with the same amused skepticism he gave to the "heathen conjurin's" —making it all seem unimportant, as indeed it was to the life of the place, and Barber lacked the information to beat down his objections.

"They was a professor down to Harvard proved a steamboat couldn't hold enough wood to take it 'cross the ocean," he would say with an air of finality, and getting out a very homemade banjo, chanted rather than sang, in a raucous nasal tenor:

> *"It was the brilliant autumn time*
> *When the army of the north*
> *With its cannon and dragoons*
> *And its riflemen came forth.*

> *"Through the country all abroad*
> *There was spread a mighty fear*
> *Of the Indians in the van*
> *And the Hessians in the rear . . ."*

Or they would sit above a board through a long evening, drinking berry wine and playing nine-man morris. It was a game combining features of checkers and tit-tat-toe, for which Fawcett had whittled out an elaborate set of pieces. Barber found himself a hopeless dub at it, but this did not seem to matter to Fawcett, who treated the game, and almost everything else, as a background for endless conversations on Jacksonian politics or experiences with the heathen. Life rolled smoothly; Oberon, the war, his former existence were lapped deep in the wave of the past, and it might not be too bad to slide forever through this region of perfect peace.

Or almost perfect. There was the incident of the broken hoe. Both men were engaged in what Fawcett called "cultivatin'" a field of potatoes, an operation that seemed singularly pointless to Barber, as it consisted in no more than digging vigorously with a hoe at the base of the young plants, piling the earth half an inch deeper around the stalks. "Make's a neat field," was Fawcett's only answer to Barber's protest that the few sprigs of grass rooted up in the process could be of no importance to the potatoes, which grew underground in any case. "Good farmers have neat fields."

As he brought his hoe down in a particularly vigorous sweep to emphasize some conversational point he was making, the farmer struck a subsoil rock and the blade snapped off at the shank. He clucked annoyance over the small disaster. "Guess I'shall have to make another hoss trade with the mountain heathen," he remarked, when he had replaced the instrument with another from the house. "Ain't got but three hoes to the hull place. That's funny, too, now I call it to mind. They ain't been 'round for a right smart spell; usually you can't keep 'em away, specially when they know I'been makin' berry wine. They'd most trade their eyeteeth out for berry wine."

He trailed off into an anecdote illustrative of the kobolds' appetite for berry wine, and next morning after breakfast dug out a big blue-and-white flag on the end of a stick and affixed it to the roof of the house, explaining that this was the signal he wanted to trade with the kobolds. Barber wondered whether there would be any of the gang he had encountered among the traders, but he might have spared himself the worry. No kobolds came that day or the next. The second night Fawcett exhibited a trace of concern across the supper table.

"Dunno what's come over 'em; maybe they're waxed at me 'bout suthin'. They have mighty ungainly idears about what's right, those mountain heathen, and when a man won't go 'long with 'em, they set in the seats of the scornful. But I should hate to lose their trade; ain't been any hardware peddler through this way since I'come. A man can't farm without tools."

"I could go look them up and find out what's wrong," offered Barber tentatively.

"By George, that's right! Them mountain heathen is choosy as all git out 'bout lettin' people into their place, but I fergit you was a perfessional ambassador to increase perfumes afar off in the sight of the Lord, like it says in fifty-seven Isaiah. Tell you what, mister; I shall give you a jug of berry wine in the mornin' and you mosey up there."

Barber was already repenting his overready suggestion, but there was no decent method of withdrawing, and next day he set out across the little belt of upland rolling to the Kobold Hills. As he went he became more than ever regretful over having let himself in for this piece of foolishness. The day was already hot and the wine jug burdensome; he could not but contrast his present toiling gate with the easy lightfootedness of his previous journey. As a matter of fact, it was even slower and more difficult than it should have been. Made thus, as a reversed experience, the journey underlined something of which he had been uncomfortably, but only vaguely, conscious for some time: that he felt definitely less well than he had before.

No, "felt" was the wrong verb, he assured himself,

realizing with the other, critical half of his brain that the ceaseless flow of Fawcett's chatter had kept him from introspection for weeks. And through it from localizing the trouble. He "felt" like a prize bull pup, now that he came to examine the question; his sensations with regard to the world about him were of extreme enjoyment. If he could have been translated back to the Embassy he would have plunged into the compilation of official reports with positive delight.

In short, he felt swell. It was the physical equipment which accompanied his feelings that seemed to be showing deterioration. He had not realized it till undertaking this long hike, but it was actually growing difficult for him to walk. His legs were stiff, and was it mere hypochondriac imagination or had they acquired a tendency to bow? No, he decided, pausing on the last rise but one to catch his breath and gaze at the offending limbs, it was not hypochondria. The other manifestation was real enough; his feet had spread, grossly and outrageously. The shoes made by the royal tailor he had been forced to discard at the end of the first week at Fawcett's. Now he was wearing a pair of the farmer's enormous boots, and even these, which had begun by fitting him like bedroom slippers, were now pinching him painfully.

There was something wrong with his eyes, too. When not consciously focused on something they had a tendency to roll outward—not painful, but noticeable when he discovered that he was seeing double. It must be some kind of allergy or vitamin deficiency, he decided. Diet might be responsible; it included a plenitude of fresh vegetables, but was lacking in the familiar dairy products and in any meat but the venison which Fawcett secured by trading with the heathen. Acromegaly, Barber presumed his ailment might be called, but the prescription for it he did not know. At all events it appeared to have the compensating benefit of causing those absurd shoulder-blade wings of his to stop growing. They had actually shrunk an inch or two.

. . . He was at the entrance of the caverns, the same, as near as he could judge, by which he had left. All dark inside, and now that he noticed it, all silent, too; not a sound of forge or hammer, in waltz time or any other. Very dark; he was reminded of a lecture in his college physics class: "The only complete black in nature is a hole in the ground." It seemed absurd to plunge into that well of night, equally absurd to turn back without trying it. After a moment more of ir-resolution, he gathered force and took the step, feeling along the wall with one hand.

The wall was slightly damp, and the deeper he went the more he cursed himself for a fool—with no light or Ariadne's clue to bring him out again. He started counting his steps, trying to keep them even in length, which would be at least some help. . . . Twenty-two, twenty-three, twenty-four—he paused, turned and looked back at the shield of light. Still there. . . . A hundred and forty-nine, a hundred and fifty—he turned again, saw the light spot smaller, and wished he had started counting at the very mouth of the tunnel. Somewhere ahead there was a small sound—tap, tap, tap, which, after a moment's agonized attention, he identified as the dripping of water.

A hundred yards more—and the supporting wall at his right suddenly disappeared, so that he went sprawl-ing. Branch in the tunnel. It brought him face to face with the problem of carrying on, through those blind, involuted galleries. No, certainly not worth it, without lights and no sign of life. He compromised by standing at the angle for a moment and shouting. There was no answer but the monotonous drip, drip, drip of the subterranean water. After waiting a few more hopeless moments he turned and groped his way back.

When he reached the mouth of the cavern, the morning's faint overcast had turned to cloud and persistent, drizzling rain that felt delightful after the heat. Fawcett was nowhere visible as Barber trudged across the rises toward the homestead. Neither was the horse, Federalist, which probably meant that the farmer had ridden up the stream to indulge in his favorite rainy-day sport of conducting a trade with the forest natives.

Barber went into the house and upstairs to a room that was used relatively rarely. Fawcett had furnished it with unusual elaboration, even to window curtains of his own manufacture and in materials that had probably never been used for curtaining before. That brocade, for example, might have come from the upholstery of the Escorial. It was the sturdy Yank's one touch of sentiment, the one indication that he might harbor the thought of a partnership in this wilderness. Barber had found him curiously reticent on the point except when the farmer delivered one of his occasional tirades on the habits of the heathen.

"Them women, now," he would say, waving his mug of wine. "Some of 'em are purty as a pitcher; look like good workers, too. But they skrawk round like chick turkeys with the pip till a man could chaw the wall. They have a superstition; you say suthin' to 'em, and accordin' to their rules, they's only two-three replies they can make. Blessed if I want a woman that has a law of the Medes and Persians to make her say 'Good mornin' every time I say 'Howdedo.' "

. . . Barber jumped to his feet, with a sudden horror embracing him. When he had come into that room and seated himself in the homemade rocking chair, there had certainly been a pair of flies cruising about the ceiling. The door was closed, and the windows, but the flies were no longer there—

And Barber could remember distinctly that, while

he had been meditating on Fawcett's sentimental spot, he had once—twice—shot a hand out, with the ease of reflex action, and put it to his mouth.

The fear that he was going insane leaped on him again, enforced and redoubled. What else could make him do a thing like that? Perhaps it was even a part of the delusion that his legs were bowing and his hips seemed to have acquired a sudden "middle-aged squat"; perhaps—whoa, that wasn't it, either. There was no reasonable doubt about the changed size of his feet; Fawcett himself had remarked on it when lending him the boots. Something had just gone wrong, badly wrong with his whole physical make-up.

He began to pace the floor in agitation, hunting for the answer, then paused with a flash of recollection. It was his own fault. He had allowed himself to sink into the contentment of this farm. But it was not the discovery of the good life, it was old-fashioned shirking. The venture into the Kobold Caverns had been only half his task. However completely he had brought to an end their swordmaking—through no great address of his own—there remained the second duty of returning Titania's wand. He had tried to forget it by escaping into Fawcett's clocklike existence, but the responsibility remained. Whatever had gone wrong with him would probably, nay, certainly, grow worse till he finished his job. In fact, it might continue until he found his way back to England and sanity along the same route he had traveled to reach this place. It was the "misadventured piteous overthrow" the Queen had promised.

And how was he to finish that job? How find his way back through the caverns, across the desert and to the Plum who had taken that confounded stick? Damn it! He kicked at air in irritation over the unfairness of everything. Why did all these Fairyland people have to be so vague? Fawcett was the only one in the lot capable of a definite statement, and now Barber was being forced to leave him behind.

For that was what it amounted to. Wherever that needlelike wand was in this immense vague haystack of a country, whatever handicaps his splay-footed, bow-legged, wall-eyed condition imposed upon Barber, it was clear he would have to get away from that farm and go searching. The excuses he could make to himself were unlikely to be convincing to this case of galloping jimjams from which he was suffering.

A sound outside made him step to the window. Fawcett was riding into the yard, with rain dripping from his own hat and the horse's mane, an expression of pleasure on his sideburned face. The trading expedition had evidently been a success; across his saddle-bow was a large and bulging bag, incongruously made of cloth of gold, with the handle of something sticking out of it. It occurred to Barber that the last thing in the world he wanted was to explain his plight to that cold-eyed and skeptical New Englander. He took three quick steps across the room, flung open the door, and dashed into his own room. The sword he had brought was there; he snatched it up, went down the stairs three at a time, and gazed from the kitchen window. Fawcett had just dismounted, and was leading Federalist into the sod-house barn.

Barber stepped quickly to the door of the kitchen-living room and out, slipped round the house to put it between him and the farmer, and started off. He looked back now and then, changing direction slightly to keep the bulk of the buildings between him and the house, and so angling away from the Kobold Hills. The rain felt good on his face.

Not till he was passing among the first sentinels of a line of trees did he remember the Kobold caves again and the fact that he was leaving Fawcett in quite genuine trouble, with his supply of iron tools cut off. However, there was nothing that he, Barber, could do about it in his present condition and with more urgent business on hand. If he found the wand and returned to Oberon with it, perhaps that monarch would do something for the farmer. Perhaps he would be able to send Barber back where he belonged.

If he found the wand.

CHAPTER XI

The trees drew in around him to form an extensive grove. Big, slow drops slipped from their branches, and the going was heavy. But when Barber glanced aloft he saw a streak of blue among the clouds, and by the time he had reached the far side of the tree belt the sun broke through to shine down, clear and bright, as though nature itself were smiling on his resolution to take the road again. Here the ground pitched down across a meadow of rank grass toward a watercourse—probably the river to which Fawcett had occasionally referred. He pushed toward it, the grasses clutching at his ankles. No breath of wind stirred; and the summer sun was blistering hot as postlude to the shower.

The river ran on sluggishly, not much wider than that in *the* forest, spreading into a pool where Barber paused on its bank in the shade of a tall poplar. There was yellow sand on the bottom, spotted with dead leaves, cool and inviting in its rippled refraction. Nothing else moved but a pair of dragonflies patrolling over the pool, intent on their own particular brand of murder, and a kingfisher diving like a Stuka from a branch downstream.

Barber paused, one hand on the poplar trunk, contemplating the dragonflies, and realized he was hungry. When they flew in opposite directions his eyes swung out on independent orbits, one following each of the insects, and his appetite increased.

Hell, he was getting to the stage of wanting to eat

dragonflies. Titania's "overthrow" was affecting his mind as well as his body, giving him one of those psychoses that made people swallow handfuls of thumbtacks or broken bottles. What was more, his skin had developed an exasperating sensitivity, ever since the morning's rain. He stirred uneasily in clothes that rasped, and wondered whether the effect of the sudden sun on dampened garments had something to do with it.

What he needed was a swim. Maybe that would snap him out of it.

He peered along the line of poplars, saw no one and nothing, and undressed with fumbling haste. Let's see—he didn't want to leave his clothes in a heap on the brink, nor yet to take chances with the sword. He rolled both up into a single bundle, rammed the package under some spreading ferns, and dropped a dead branch over the cache to help out the camouflage.

The poplar roots had assembled enough earth around themselves to make a little hummock at the edge of the pool. He stood erect on it for a moment, stretched comfortably, took a deep breath and dove.

No shock. As soon as he was well under water he opened his eyes. The thought flashed across his mind without conscious phrasing that this was the strangest swim or the strangest water that he had ever been in. There was curiously no feeling of wetness. Below him lay the mottled yellow-and-brown bottom, clear and bright, but much farther down than it had looked from above. He might almost have been floating through an aqueous atmosphere in one of those Freudian dreams of wingless flight. There was the same sensation of movement without effort or volition.

He drew up his legs and kicked, in the strong underwater stroke that should carry him out across the pool to the surface. The drive shot him forward above the bottom at such alarming speed that he backed water, and with a flashing sensation of surprise, he found himself hanging suspended over nothingness.

At the same moment he realized that he had really been under long enough to come up for air, but that his lungs were not protesting in the least, he was getting along without man's most intimate necessity in perfect comfort. Whatever Fairyland metamorphosis he had undergone was not without its compensations.

> *"Nothing of him that doth fade,*
> *But doth suffer a sea-change*
> *Into something rich and strange . . ."*

he repeated to himself, and thinking inconsequentially of Kingsley's *Water Babies,* ducked his head down and swam cautiously lower. No difficulties. He tried another powerful kick, and the bottom rushed up at him as though he were falling from a skyscraper window. He hit it at an angle and bounced, tumbling head over heels, in a cloud of fine sand that obscured his vision. As it settled, with the larger flakes corkscrewing slowly past, he picked himself up and felt for bumps.

There seemed to be nothing damaged. Standing on tiptoe, he launched out again and found himself once more soaring over the bottom in that strange wingless flight, sustained by the surrounding medium. It must be as graceful to watch as it was easy to perform.

A silvery titter of laughter floated to him from above, right and rear. Barber spun round.

"Kaja!" he cried.

A slim, red-haired girl was drifting easily, twenty feet from him. She made a slight paddling motion and slid easily into position beside him.

"Sorry, old dear," she said, "but the name's Cola. Or Arvicola, if you want to be formal, which I don't think. You do look so fonny, swimming like that."

Even her voice had a trace of accent, like Kaja's, but what Barber caught was the insult to his swimming. He hated being ridiculous.

"What's the matter with my swimming?"

"For a frog your age? About as elegant as a drowning beetle. You must have been a lovely tadpole."

Barber raised an eyebrow. Kaja had been like that, too—always with a note of jeering banter, as though nothing life had to offer were worth the taking. "Did you say a frog?"

"Yes, froggy." She laughed again.

Barber looked down. "First time I ever heard of a frog with hair on his chest," he remarked practically.

"Gahn." The derisive word had the note of the London streets, and then her voice turned ladylike again. "You froggies aren't veddy clever, are you? And no wonder, coming out of eggs."

Barber remained good-humored. "All right, then, I'm a frog, you newt."

Her eyes—they were green eyes—seemed to snap. "I'll thank you to be civil. After all, we voles belong to the higher orders, as though you didn't know."

He tried to bow and did a curious flip in the re-straining medium, which rather ruined his effect. "Oh, yes. And I suppose you were a baroness once. Isn't that usual with water rats?"

There was another and harder snap to her eyes. "Listen," she said, "I don't know why I take the trouble to stay here and be insulted, and I won't, either, if you carry on that way. The next time you call me a water rat—"

"I'm sorry," said Barber, and was. "I didn't mean to insult you. I was just carrying on your joke about frogs—and er, voles."

"Joke!" She laughed aloud, her head came forward and a pair of green eyes searched his. "Poor frog, I see now. You're new, and don't know the Laws of the Pool yet. Come with me."

A warm hand gave his a tug, and she shot off, slanting upward She was half concealed in a dimness that
began in the middle distance before Barber whipped
up his muscles to start after her, and for the first few
strokes he followed a receding pale blob. But he was
pleased to note that, once started, he gained fast, and
by time they reached the silvery, rippling overhead
he was up with her.

Barber scrambled out of the water on all fours. He
half turned to where he expected his lovely companion
to be and opened his mouth to say, "You see—"

A deep, reverberating croak was all that came out.

Barber made a frantic effort to stand up, and fell
forward on his chin. Or rather, on his lower lip. He
had no chin.

He looked down and saw a pair of thick, stubby
arms, covered with speckled skin. They ended in a
pair of hands with four widespread fingers and no
thumb. The change was complete. He was a frog, all
right.

A few feet away a rodent of about his own size sat
on the edge of the pool, her wide, luminous eyes and

sharply chiseled features bearing the same sub-human resemblance to Kaja that an ape often has to a mick. What color its fur was he could not tell, for the picture registered by his widely diverging eyes was one of blacks, whites and grays. He was colorblind.

His mouth felt funny, with the skin fitting tightly over the bones of his jaws and the queer long tongue hinged front instead of rear, for flipping at insects. This was an overthrow for fair; how could he find the wand now? What could he do? Hang around the pond till some hungry snake or snapping turtle caught up with him? He emitted a mournful croak that was intended for a groan.

The vole studied him for a moment with bright, amused eyes, lifted a paw in a beckoning motion, and slipped smoothly into the water.

Barber humped himself around—awkwardly, because his limbs were not articulated for any wide variety of movement—and leaped after her. He had forgotten the power in his great jumping-legs. Air whistled past in a self-created breeze as he soared far out over the water. He caught one glimpse of his own reflection, bruised by surface ripples, with great jeweled eyes, stubby arms spread, web-footed hindlegs trailing back, and then came down in a tremendous belly-whopper.

The red-haired girl was floating lazily beside him in the medium that seemed more normal than air. "Wiped your eye that time, old thing," she jeered. "You froggies are *so* clever." She cocked her pretty head and examined him with embarrassing thoroughness. "Really, you know, you should take the strong, silent and handsome line with a figure like that."

Barber looked at himself. To the eye he was again the man who had dived from under the poplar. No; he was a better man, for all the ominous imperfections of his arrival in Fairyland had vanished, including the stump wings.

"Uh-huh," he said humbly. "Look here, is there some place where we can talk? You said something about the Laws of the Pool, and I really don't know anything about them. I'd be awfully obliged—"

"Poor stupid froggy. Come on, then." She turned, and he followed her down an invisible slope that ended at a group of gigantic roots which sprang from the bottom to twist in again. Cola stretched herself along one of them with an arm bent behind her neck, and comfortably wiggled her toes. "The Laws of the Pool are these," she half-chanted: "To reverence by day the gods to which we pray—"

"Beg pardon," interrupted Barber, "but isn't that a sort of catechism you're supposed to learn? Because I'm on a mission and I hope—that is, I may not stay here long, so most of it wouldn't be much use to me."

The eyes widened and she lifted her head to gaze at him again. "Oh, re-ahlly," with a galling note of incredulity. "A froggy with a mission! For Sir Lacomar, I presume?"

"No. For King Oberon, if you must know."

"The Father of the Gods? Don't try to come it over me, froggy."

"What do you mean, Father of the Gods? He's no different from you or me."

"Oh, why do you have to be so stupid! Didn't I just take you to the surface? . . . But wait, you're new. Listen, poor foolish froggy; the gods can walk in air and not change. . . . Though I don't believe that tradition about them punishing evildoers by catching them and beating them. Not half. They jolly well do take some of us away, but *I* think it's mostly those they like and want to translate to their own sphere. They took Rana the other day, and she never did anything wrong in her life. . . . It would be wonderful to be made into a god."

"Oh. Isn't there any way it can happen without being taken from the pool?"

"Only when the redbeard comes. That's part of the Laws of the Pool, you know:

> '*When the redbeard comes again,*
> *Then shall fairies turn to men—*'"

She sang it to the same tune Malacea had used when she disappeared into the forest, then broke off suddenly and became practical:

"What about the other Laws, froggy? Want them or no? I haven't all day."

"My name's not froggy; it's Fred Barber. And I'd be awfully obliged if you could tell me one or two things. Perhaps I could learn more that way. For instance, I'm hunting for a wand that belongs to Queen Titania. It was stolen from me. Have you any idea where it could be?" If she laughed at him again, he was ready to give up hope.

But she didn't. "That mission again, frog—Fred?" she said, with a bantering air that carried no sting, and frowned thought. "I re-ahlly don't know unless—unless—"

"Go on."

"Come closer," said Cola.

He did so and leaned over to catch the words she was barely whispering: "Unless the Low One has it. They say he gets everything sooner or later."

"Who is the Low One?"

She lifted her head and looked around before replying. "That's what everyone asks. It's in the Laws:

> '*You shall not speak of the Low One*
> *Or question his right to rule;*
> *Lest it come on you to be numbered*
> *Among the cursed of the Pool*'—

Oh!" She put her hands to her face. "Perhaps I've done the forbidden thing just talking about Him, and the gods will punish me. I don't know why I did—"

"Have you ever seen him?"

"Please, don't." Little lines of strain and tragedy set in the vole's delicate face. She went on, so low he could hardly hear: "If he really has the wand of the Mother of Gods, there's no limit to what he can do."

"Where does he live?"

She said: "You don't want to go there, Fred. Nobody does."

"Yes, I do. If he's got that wand I'm going to get it."

"What a brave froggy!" But her voice was shaky. "You couldn't get it. You couldn't do anything. Please, Fred, listen to me. You're not talking about doing anything fine, but just something stupid—and ignorant."

"Then you won't tell me."

"No."

He stood up. How like Kaja she was! They had quarreled this way a dozen times, but every time he yielded she had despised him for her very victory. That was why— "Okay, young lady," he said, "then I'll have to ask somebody else."

"You're not really going?"

"Right this minute."

"But, Fred—" The green eyes were desperate, and then her expression changed. "All right, then, go! You don't even know the Laws, you silly helpless frog! You'll get what's coming to you, and I hope you do!" She was off the root and stamping in vexation, lovelier and more like Kaja than ever.

"I'll find someone to tell me about them."

"Who? There's only old Sir Lacomar, the mutton-headed old pot, and he's so busy watching the mussels he won't even speak to you."

Further argument seemed useless. Barber poised to take off, then felt the old tug Kaja always brought to his heartstrings, the old fascination that would never

quite let him play the game to win. He turned. "If
I stay," he said, "will you—"

"No! I never want to see you again, you—you bloody
bahstard!"

As Barber kicked himself away and soared easily
through the water, she was suddenly shaken with
sobs.

CHAPTER XII

Keeping quite close to the bank, he went on for a distance that seemed like a couple of miles but was probably much less. At this point he saw something moving down and to the left in the murky distance. As he approached, it resolved itself into a man, pulling a crude hand plow across the bottom.

The man glanced up at Barber, dropped his plow, snatched at a huge shield that hung down his back by a strap around his neck, flopped himself down and pulled the shield over him. The protection was complete. He even managed to tuck his toes out of sight.

"Hey!" said Barber, lighting beside the shield. It remained motionless.

Barber sat down to wait. This was most unlikely to be anything but one of the mussels.

In due time the shield shifted a trifle, an eye peeked out and was followed by a head. The head was apparently satisfied, for the mussel heaved the shield up and himself after it. "Thought you was a trout," he remarked by way of apology. He was stocky, muscular, stoop-shouldered, with high cheekbones and a dead-white skin, hairless as a fish.

Barber said: "Hello. My name's Barber."

"Call me Joe," said the mussel.

"Nice little farm you have here."

"Okay," said the mussel. "I got a farm. So what?"

"Nothing. I just wondered if you were one of Sir Lacomar's people."

Joe spat, the spittle drifting off to dissolution. He jerked a thumb toward the riverbank. "Awright. I work for Lacomar. And I think he's a jerk, a lousy slave driver. So what?"

"Nothing. I was looking for someone else. Can you tell me where the Low One lives?"

The mussel stuck his head forward. "Smart guy, huh? You frogs are all smart guys. He's a goddam heel, but he'll fix your wagon."

"Why? Is he coming this way?"

"Me, I wouldn't know. I just plow."

"Would it make any difference to you if he did?"

"Prob'ly not." Barber knew the mussel was not sure whether he was lying or not. "You get rid of one boss, you get another. It's all part of the system. Skip it, Mac, skip it." He jerked his thumb toward another mussel, who was dragging his plow. "If anyone takes a poke at us, we know what to do, see? Meanwhilst we don't shoot our mouths off to every lug that comes along, see?"

"I might be able to do something for you."

"You?" The mussel's deep-set eyes were scornful. "Hah! I know—gimme some literchure, work twelve hours more a day, so Lacomar, the lousy stinker, can live on pie."

Barber persisted: "Aren't you afraid of what'll happen if the Low One comes?"

"Not specially." He lied. Even without the special sense he had acquired in Fairyland Barber could have detected the undercurrent of fear. So did Joe, the mussel, and rushed on into explanation: "The system's all wrong, see? It's gotta be put through the wringer before we get a right break and maybe he's the only guy can do it."

"Isn't it against the Laws of the Pool to talk the way you have about Sir Lacomar and the Low One? What if I told on you? Though of course I won't if you give me a little information." Barber rather hated to do it, but he had to find out.

"So, you're a snitch, a agent provocateur? My word against yours, funny-face. Gwan, now beat it, before I dust you off, you goon." The mussel slung his shield over his back and glumly set off, dragging his plow.

Barber soared up and looked round. There were two or three other mussels in sight, each stonily pulling at a plow, but their expressions promised no less surly reception than that he had received from Joe, and he headed toward the bank.

Sure enough, there was where it began to slope up, a circular tower of rough stones. On the top of this tower, with his feet hanging down, sat a bulbous, ruddy-faced man. He was nearly bald, with prominent, china-blue eyes and a handle-bar mustache.

Barber swam for the top of the tower and hung suspended. "Hello," he said.

"Hello, froggy," said the ruddy man.

"The name's Barber."

"Barber, eh? Relative of the barbels? Good fellas, stout fighters. They bear azure and argent, barrywavy of six. What's your arms? Wait, I forget; frogs aren't armigerous. All poets; no fight in 'em."

"Mind if I sit awhile?"

"Not at all, old chap. Saw one of your musical relatives the other day—what was his name? Hylas. Thought his singing very nice, though I don't pretend to understand such things. Soldiers don't get much time."

Barber sat down on the parapet. He noted that a pile of plate armor lay behind the big man. "You're Sir Lacomar, aren't you?" he asked.

"Right."

"Miss Arvicola suggested I look you up."

"Oh, you know Cola? Splendid girl." Sir Lacomar held out a large red hand to be shaken. "Bit wild and free with her tongue. Don't know that I blame her, though, seeing the devil of a time she's had with You-know-who. Glad I've been able to do a favor or two for her."

"When was this?"

"Don't know the details, and naturally wouldn't ask unless the lady chose to volunteer. In my position. Should think it would make a good poem for you, though, if you could get her to tell you."

The audience was friendly but the matter had better be approached gradually. Barber asked for local news.

Sir Lacomar said: "A few things, here and there. The usual. Trout made a raid from one of the tributaries last week. Got poor old Krebitz, but we routed 'em handsomely."

"Oh. One of your fellow crawfish?"

"Naturally. Splendid chap; one of the Astak family, who bear argent a blood-ax gules. Very old line, but he was a younger son and had to difference it. I remember the time Krebitz and Sir Karkata and I drove a whole tribe of bullheads from the Muddy Pool. They were lined up like this, y'see—" he illustrated with a string of pebbles—"when we took 'em in the flank and then, Santiago for the red and white! I say, that was a real fight. I lost an arm."

Barber looked at Sir Lacomar's two muscular arms.

"Came off near the shoulder," Lacomar went on, without noticing, "and that's always a bad business. Had to go into retreat for months while I was growing the new one. Don't know who'll take the war-cry and the profit after Krebitz; young Cambarus, most likely. He's the old man's sister's grandson. But an unlicked whelp—an unlicked whelp; never been blooded, and he has no real right to be Warden of the Inner March, because that doesn't pass in the female line. I suppose Scudo will put in his claim and then You-know-who will want to arbitrate."

"Are you people going to let him?"

"Hah! Not without putting up the standard and giving Him the battle of his life. That's His way of getting a foot in the door. Did it with the trout in the West Reach, you know. Not that anyone minded what happened to the crew of damned pirates. Served 'em right."

"Didn't they fight?"

"Tried. But they were disorganized, d'you see, and had no proper weapons. Not like us. Besides, the gods took their chief, Christy, just as the attack started. They're always just."

"Perhaps," said Barber, "they were less interested in Christy's character than in his edibility."

Sir Lacomar's face froze a trifle. "Now, now, young fella, don't blaspheme. All very well to talk that way among your fellow poets, and personally, I quite understand you have to be a little loose in your morals, keep up the artist's life, eh? Sowed a few wild oats myself, once. But it simply won't do if you want to be taken up by the right people. Sort of thing a mussel would say."

"Thanks, I'll watch it," said Barber humbly. "They're not very well brought up, are they?"

The knight snorted. "Wouldn't do 'em any good if they were. Education, my boy, is something for which the masses are not fitted. Like trying to make a sword out of a piece of wood; must have a bit of the right stuff first. What they need is a spot of discipline. Now, mind you—" he shook a finger under Barber's nose—"I'll grant What's-his-name is no gentleman, and He gave little Cola a pretty thin time of it. But you must admit He does know how to make His own people look sharp. He'll turn them into something yet, mark my word. Wouldn't do my mussels any harm to have a bit of that treatment, the ungrateful beggars. Risk life and limb for 'em, give 'em sound government and stability, and what d'you get? A deputation to ask for more holidays!" Another snort expressed Sir Lac-omar's supreme contempt for holidays, and he caressed his mustache with energy. "*We* can't afford to take holidays. What if the trout came down on a raid the afternoon we chose for a little outing? Would the mussels defend us? Turnabout's fair play and fair play's a jewel, I always say."

The crawfish-knight was actually puffing in his in-dignation and Barber judged it prudent to change the subject. "You know," he said, "I'm on rather a serious mission as it happens. I'm looking for a piece of property that belongs to the Mother of the Gods, and I've been led to believe it might be in Whoozis' possession. Could you suggest how I might go about recovering it?"

Sir Lacomar frowned. "Don't know about that, my boy. I hardly think You-know-who would violate prop-erty rights. Not His style; too big for that sort of thing, if you understand."

"All the same I'd like to look into it. Where does Thingumbob keep himself?"

"Nobody knows but Cola, and she doesn't tell. You might ask the leeches. They're subjects of His."

"Where do I find them?"

"Upstream a way, where a tributary comes in from the right bank."

"Well, I think I'll go see. Good-by and thanks." Barber poised on the edge of the tower to take off.

"'By, old man, and 'ware fish. Oh, by the way, I'd be grateful if you'd look into His methods a little. Interested in finding out how He achieves such order."

As Barber swam upstream, a vague general malaise told him, more through instinct than reason, that he needed another breath of air. He slid easily upward and his eyes broke surface into that dead, black-and-white world which faded into a blur at any distance. Like stepping into a worn, old-fashioned movie. An insect rocketed past, and one eye followed it unbidden, but its appearance did not telegraph "food" to his sphincters as those of the dragonflies had before he plunged into the life of the Pool. Perhaps it was just as well that he had lost the desire for that form of nourishment; an adjustment that had brought his world more into harmony with his own temperament and the inherited human taboos.

But it did set him wondering about the dietetic arrangements of the underwater people. He had not felt hungry yet and was not now—what would he do when he was? Before he could achieve any speculation on the question his eye caught the fleeting movement of a shadow on the bottom as he propelled himself through the atmosphere—hydrosphere—with easy, powerful strokes, and it occurred to him that his froggishness had made him not too ill-adapted to this new environment. Compare it with the world above, he told himself smugly. Like the daring young man on the flying trapeze, he could sail through the skies above such earth-bound agrarians as the mussels. Or even Sir Lacomar, probably. He experienced a surge of pity for that hardy veteran of the limited outlook. Brave Sir Lacomar, I sympathize; but you cannot, like me, ride the airs with Kaja-Cola.

In fact, he might do worse than stay there beneath the silvery, tight-fitting surface with that tempestuous and lovely—vole. The word brought the meditation to a halt. He was an interloper in this submarine world, more separate from her thought and way of life than Barber of the Embassy had been from Kaja, of Budapest or Soho. It wouldn't do; it wouldn't do even if he could abandon his origins to live her life, under the Laws of the Pool. For that matter, he could not abandon those origins. It was an attempt to do that, at Fawcett's farm, that had brought him here, produced the mutation. Correct enough for the Yank, who had another and different destiny to fulfill, as the life of the submarine world was the dish for Cola.

He, Barber the frog, the Barber of Seville, would only risk another, unhappier metamorphosis by the attempts to share their tasks and contentments when he was geared for other, more difficult jobs.

No escape except upward, then; no path but the hard and hateful one of a duty he had not sought. For that matter, which he did not even know how to perform. He remembered with dismay a tag from old Nietzsche: "He who cannot find the way to his ideal lives more shamelessly than the man without an ideal." The most and best he could do was carry on.

"Good morning! Good afternoon! Good evening!" called a voice. Barber looked down to find himself just moving past the entrance of a tributary so hidden in reeds that he might have missed it altogether but for the sound. He banked and planed down beside the curious-looking individual who had called out. Like the mussels, he was innocent of hair. Forehead and chin receded from a sharp-nosed, vacuous face whose mouth was set in a mechanical grin; there was a nice, sun-tan brown around the grin, but whenever the individual moved it became evident that his back was green, a sharp dividing line running down arms and ribs.

A limp boneless hand was thrust into Barber's. "Welcome to Hirudia!" said the individual, with energy. "Welcome to the land of order and plenty!"

CHAPTER XIII

"Can you tell me where I can find the leeches?" Barber said. "Unless you're one of them."

"Of course I'm a leech, and proud of it!" Green-back whistled sharply, and from among the reed columns was joined by three more, bearing to him the same maddening resemblance that Chinese have for each other. All bowed. "Visitors are welcome to Hirudia, sir! We are honored to escort you—an unforgettable experience."

The last phrase was a trifle ambiguous, and Barber found the welcome a disturbing parody of that he had received in the Kobold Hills. "Well, I don't know that I want to go that far," he said. "Perhaps you could give me the information I want."

"Certainly, sir. It would give us the greatest pleasure."

"Very well. Can you tell me where the Low One lives?"

The leeches looked at each other, their expressions changing. They drew off a few steps and put their heads together—whisper, whisper. After a moment or two the first one came back, his face bland. "We're very sorry, indeed, sir, but we are not allowed to discuss political matters. There are certain regulations, as I'm sure you'll understand. But if you would care to step into Hirudia, the Boss could inform you. The Boss knows everything."

"Who is your Boss?"

"Why, he's our father and mother! It was the Boss who rescued us from weakness and disorganization, and co-ordinated us into our present state of order and progress. He keeps us safe from the depredations of the trout, and protects us from the encirclement of the crawfish. A wonderful person! So modest and intelligent! We'd do anything for the Boss."

There was something not altogether reassuring about this avowal, the more so since Barber's lie-detecting sense gave him no intimation that the leeches were telling anything but the truth. He hoped the Boss was as good-natured as he seemed to be admired. In any case the leeches were undersized, flabby creatures, visibly weaponless. If it came to another Kobold Cavern difficulty, he could handle a dozen of them—and he held here an advantage he had never held there. He could leap up; swim away at a speed he was certain the leeches could not match.

A sense of confidence in his own powers enveloped him as he followed the first leech, with the other three behind. The leader chattered continuously over his shoulder. "Hirudia has become a changed place since our Boss arrived. You wouldn't recognize it. Everything systematic, the work done so easily and efficiently. The rest of the world will someday learn to appreciate us, whom they have neglected. We cannot remain forever hemmed in among the reeds."

"Hm," said Barber. "And what's your personal part in this, if I may ask?"

"Me? Oh, I have leisure."

"You have leisure?"

"Certainly. Take the mussels, for instance. They live in one of the old-fashioned, competitive communities, where economic pressure forces everyone to endless and hopeless labor." He rattled this off like a train of cars going over a switch, then paused and added proudly: *"Our* Boss assigns certain of us to the duty of having leisure. We take it outside the city,

where passers-by can see us and know the lies that are
told about our beautiful land for what they are. That
is social justice."

"Do you have leisure twenty-four hours a day?"

"Of course. There is no time wasted in Hirudia.
The competitive communities are monuments to inefficiency and waste."

"I should think you'd get bored," said Barber, holding to the point.

"Bored? Oh, no! Boredom is a product of the class
system and social disintegration. One never gets bored
in Hirudia. It would be disloyalty to the achievements
of our Boss."

The answer was glib as ever and the tone un-
changed, but a red light burned within Barber's mind,
signifying "lie." Not surprising; he had heard of pro-
grams of enforced leisure before, only usually they
were called something else.

They wound through alleys of tall reed trunks, like
the pillars of Karnak, till they reached a wall which
stretched up and sidewise to the limit of vision. The
leading leech whistled, up scale and down, and a section of the wall sprang open without visible agency.
Behind it was another wall, with a narrow slit
through which an eye scrutinized them suspiciously
before this wall too, opened, but in a different place.
Beyond it the guiding leech whistled again, another
tune, before a third wall—and then came another and
another and another, alternately guarded by eye and
ear, till Barber lost count.

"For a model community," he remarked, "you take
unusual care in matters of fortification."

"We must protect ourselves from the jealousy of
our neighbors. An enlightened and progressive nation
is always an island in the midst of a sea of enemies."

A last well opened to reveal an immense plaza
where reed trunks grew from the bottom, but in strict
geometrical rows with open spaces between. Many

more leeches were in sight, all alike as eggs, and all furiously busy. Just to the left of the gate a group of three were building a narrow tower of bricks. One brought the bricks from a pile, a second sat at the top of the tower, hauling them up in a basket, while the third laid the bricks. Barber observed that the tower was not really a tower, but a solid, square monolith without openings or exterior features.

"What's that for?" he asked his guide.

"I don't know, sir, but it has social importance or it would not have been ordered by our Boss. In enlightened ages all the public works have social importance. Foreigners should not inquire into the actions of the co-operative state without full knowledge of their ultimate social purpose."

It was the same rapid flow of sententious vocables as before, like a lesson learned by rote, but the last sentence was subtly tinged with insolence—now they were inside the walls. Barber glanced at him sharply. "The purpose is what I was trying to find out," he observed. "May I ask the workers?"

The four leeches drew apart and consulted, whisper, whisper again, and their leader came back. "Unlike the decadent feudalisms, Hirudia has nothing to hide. We shall be glad to have you ask any worker anything."

The next time the brick carrier appeared with his hod, Barber inquired: "Beg pardon, but could you tell me what this brick thing is?"

The leech leaned his hod against the tower and began heaving bricks into the basket at a furious rate, whipping out a word or two at a time between heaves: "Cultural—object, sir—ordered by—the Boss."

Barber's four guides had clustered round to listen with an intentness that was almost painful, their heads stretched forward and cocked to one side. Now they exchanged smiles.

"But why are you doing the work?" persisted Barber.

"Because—I love—the Boss—would die—for him—we all—love him—excuse please." The leech had emptied the hod and filled the basket, and now trotted off. He had certainly lied; never had Barber's new sixth sense given him a clearer warning. But never, either, had there been a more bewilderingly complete lack of use for the knowledge. He decided he had been mistaken about the resemblance to the kobolds. At least that lot had been enjoying themselves.

Behind a row of the stately columns two piles of gravel lay on the bottom, several yards apart. A couple of leeches were at work on these while a third supervised. The two laborers each had a wheelbarrow and a shovel, and one was at either pile. At the supervisor's "Hup!" each would fill his wheelbarrow as fast as possible; with another "Hup!" they started toward each other's piles, pushing the barrows ahead of them. As they passed in mid-course the supervisor smiled, saying no more till each leech had emptied his wheelbarrow on the other's pile and raced back to his own for a repetition of the process.

It made even less sense, if possible, than the construction of the eyeless tower, and Barber watched the procedure for some minutes in an effort to find the key. But the routine never varied. Finally, as one of the leeches passed, Barber was driven to ask him what it was all about.

The green-and-brown mannikin continued its gallop, so that Barber had to trot back and forth beside it as it jerked out: "Aesthetic—pursuit—orders of—the Boss."

"I don't see anything very aesthetic about it," said Barber honestly.

They had reached the end of the run, and the wheelbarrow man had a moment's respite before the next "Hup." He turned a stricken face to Barber and said rapidly: "There isn't. You frogs know—you're artists. Help me get out of—"

"Hup!"

The leech's eyes leaped over Barber's shoulder, his face set in lines of fear, and he began to shovel frantically, panting out words: "Glad we—have—opportunity—for artistic—expression—unlike outworn—communities—our Boss—patron of—the arts." Barber turned and almost ran into two of the guides, who were gazing past him at the laborer, their permanent smiles twisted into peculiarly malevolent grins.

One of them took him by either arm. "This way, sir," they said in chorus. They had led him perhaps fifty yards farther down the plaza, when a short shriek behind made him turn round, the wheelbarrow of the leech with whom he had been conversing lay on its side with the gravel spilled. Of the individual there was no sign.

"What became of him?" asked Barber.

"He was tired," said one of the escorts smoothly, "so he was relieved, and sent on a vacation. Our Boss is aware of something the decadent communities have never learned; that labor is entitled to adequate recreational facilities." It was false as hell, and Barber knew it. He was getting pretty tired of glorious Hirudia, which seemed to have been developed on a pattern entirely too familiar.

He said: "I'd like very much to see more of your city, but this is more of a business trip than a visit for me. When can I see your Boss?"

"We're taking you to him," said one of the guides. At this end of the plaza, the reed columns were spaced wider, and through them there became visible buildings of a cyclopean architecture, flat, fat and squatty. They drew in till the plaza ended in a square arch at the door of one; Barber was conducted into a passage, round a turn, up one ramp and down another. Beyond was a smaller plaza and more overstuffed buildings, and so on, till he quite lost orientation. In one of these places they came to a halt, while one of the leeches went into a blocky structure.

In a surprisingly short time he was back. "The Boss is holding an important conference. Will the gentleman come with us to the place of attendance?"

"What's that?" demanded Barber, his suspicions now unappeasably aroused.

"The place where gentlemen who wish to see the Boss wait," purred the leech. "In Hirudia everything is done systematically."

"How long do they have to wait?"

"Very little time." (Lie.) "Every comfort will be at your disposal" (Lie) "and you may leave to conduct other business whenever you wish." (Lie.)

"Sorry," said Barber. "Convey my respects to your Boss and say that I regretted not having seen him, but I had business that couldn't wait. Which is the quickest way out of here?"

"Oh!" said all four leeches together. "You don't want to leave Hirudia! You haven't seen half of it! You want to come with us to the place of attendance."

"No," said Barber. "I know what I want, and that is to get out of here. Will you please—"

The leeches interrupted: "Sir, it is contrary to regulations and good sense for anyone to leave Hirudia until he fully understands it." "You cannot understand beautiful Hirudia in a few minutes." "Perhaps he's socially underdeveloped." "Needs instruction."

Barber pointed at random. He barked: "Is that the way out?"

"No," said a leech. Barber knew it was a lie, and set off in the direction indicated. The leeches followed him, yammering that he was being impulsive instead of reasonable; that he didn't want to leave Hirudia; that he hadn't seen . . .

Other leeches swarmed out of the buildings and joined the procession till there were dozens of them around and beside him, all talking at once. One worked up courage enough to grab Barber's arm. He shook the flaccid hand off angrily. The clamor grew louder.

"You can't get away, sir!" they cried. "Why try?" "You'll only cause a lot of fuss, and somebody will get hurt." "Send for the Symptosites." "Anything is better than having trouble and people getting hurt, isn't it?" "Honestly, we're nice fellows, not so different from you; why not join us?" "This is really your big chance to learn about Hirudia; it's expanding to take over the whole river in time, and you might much better join us now, when it's easy." "When you really understand us, you won't want to leave." "Don't cause a commotion, sir, please! It's so uncivilized." "You ought to be so happy over the chance to get in step with the new Laws of the Pool." "Here's a fair warning —if you provoke us to the use of force it will be all your fault." "Isn't he stupid? He thinks he can get away from all of us together."

Oh, to hell with this babble, thought Barber. He could still swim. He flexed his muscles and took off, rising over the leeches' heads and the featureless pediments of their buildings. A powerful leg kick sent him in the direction where he hoped the exit was, cursing himself for never being able to remember turns.

A bend to avoid a reed column gave him a glance rearward. The leeches were coming along behind, all right, with an undulating stroke, swimming fast, though not as fast as he was.

Something went Bong, Bong, slowly and with decision. More leeches appeared, swarming up from all directions out of the boxlike buldings. Barber dodged round a tower that reared itself above the rest, and found two right in his path, vacuous mouths open, arms spread to catch him. He gave another leg-stroke and at the same moment swung at the nearer; fist met jaw with soulful violence, and he felt the flimsy bones crumble. "Left hook!" he shouted for no reason, as the other leech dodged, wrapped itself around his leg and began to chew his calf. A kick flung it loose; beneath him legions of leeches were streaming up with out-stretched arms, while the two he had disposed of drifted away, belly-up.

Yet that brief delay had given those ahead time to get past his level, and now as Barber looked, he per-ceived he was the center of a sphere of leeches. They were closing in with evident reluctance, but closing. Where was the exit? The sphere seemed denser at one side; that was probably it, they would concentrate to keep him in. He charged in that direction. One leech, braver than the rest, stood straight across his path. He butted it amidships, and from the tail of his eye saw it turn belly-up as he kicked and punched his way through the soft, clutching things.

They gave; he sped through, dodged scattered sin-gle leeches still floating up, and found himself over the great plaza. A few foreshortened forms were visible below, one or two swimming toward him, but for the most part it was empty. He slid across it, outdistancing pursuit here in the open, feeling free at last—

Until he saw the reason. All up and down, the great wall was a solid mass of leeches. He dived toward the base of the wall, where the gate was. They gave way before his rush. No gate; the wall loomed smooth as a mirror, and around him on every side were the leeches in a hemisphere, millions of them, blotting out the light with their bodies and inching in. The surface, which might be an escape, and might not—how far did this wall go?—was far away.

Barber got his feet on the ground and his back to the wall and cocked his fists for a last-ditch struggle. Might possibly discourage them. The leeches inched in, their array thickening as the radius of the sphere lessened. Their hands spread, when the pressure of the wall against Barber's shoulder blades ceased.

He took two steps, threw a wild menacing punch to drive the nearest back, and spun to face whatever leeches were coming from behind.

It was not leeches; or rather, there were only two. Between them stood Arvicola, Sir Lacomar and another knight, the last two clad from top to toe in armor.

CHAPTER XIV

One of the newcomer leeches said: "What's this? Most unseemly; just when we are bringing visitors to admire—"

This was as far as he got. Sir Lacomar crossed his arms in front of him, fists down, and jerked them up, whipping paired broadswords out of their sheaths. They hit the two leeches simultaneously, the blades shearing deep into soft bodies. The other knight's visor came down clang; with a long, lashing blade he disemboweled a venturesome leech that dove at them from above.

"Outside, you two!" roared Lacomar. "We'll cover the bloody retreat!"

But the gates beyond were closed; and even as Barber and Arvicola turned to that inmost gate, it slid smoothly into position behind them. The four were inside Hirudia and held there.

Pressure from the constantly growing mass drove the nearest leeches, willy-nilly, in on the two knights. For a few seconds they moved in a web of whirling steel before the tide surged back amid squeals of panic fear. The water was murky with their blood and the small clear space was littered with heads, legs, arms and entrails, while the crowd above emitted a confused growling roar of mingled anger and terror.

Lacomar glanced over his shoulder. "What are you waiting for, froggy? Told you to push off."

"The gate's closed," said Barber.

Lacomar gave a little leap, and his point just caught a dangling knee. "Ha, Santiago! Open it, froggy."

"Can't. Don't know how."

The other knight boomed something that was lost in the recesses of his helmet, turned, and ran his sword along the surface of the wall behind them, searching for the joint. It gave the exquisite shriek of a pin dragged across a windowpane, but wall and gate fitted solidly. He snapped up his visor. "The frog's right," he said. "No way out."

"Tell him to produce an idea," said Lacomar, still facing out and up. "Frogs always have ideas."

"Not this one or this time," said Barber grimly. Lacomar sidestepped like a dancer as one of the leeches came sweeping in at knee level, and stabbed him through the guts. The leech screamed. "That'll teach the blighter," remarked Lacomar, with a barking laugh, "but what'll we do?"

Arvicola said, with obvious effort: "There is another way out. It—leads through His . . ."

"Good!" said Lacomar. "Show us the way, old gal."

"How about lending me one of those swords?" asked Barber. Lacomar looked surprised, then doubtful. "Be damned!" said the other knight. "A fighting frog! Here, take my anlace." He fumbled at his belt and handed Barber an object like a clove, all metal and about two feet long. It balanced well, and had dangerous-looking spikes around the head.

"Swim or walk?" asked Barber.

"Swim?" boomed the stranger-knight. "Not in this hardware." And Lacomar gave a dry chuckle. "Told you frogs always have ideas—usually wrong 'uns."

They set out, Lacomar leading with his two-sword sweep, Barber and the other knotting around Arvicola. At the third step the leeches burst into a frantic gabble of shouts and squeals: "Give up?" "Come with us—you'll be treated kindly." "You've put up enough resistance to make your showing—it will be all right, we understand good fighters." They gave no answer, and after a minute or two of talking themselves into a fury, the creatures charged again.

Barber was the center of a circle of clutching arms and biting mouths, laying about him furiously. Once Arvicola screamed and clung to his left arm; he executed a difficult pirouette with a leech clinging to his legs, and drove the anlace, once and repeat, into the faces of the pair who had her by the shoulders. They collapsed, floating away upward, but another dived in from behind to catch him by the throat and carry him to his knees. Here we go, he thought, but a voice bellowed something like "Tambo!" and the pressure was released. He scrambled to his feet, head swimming, to see the stranger-knight standing over him, and shouted. Then the fight was ended for the moment, with fragments of leech bodies drifting dejectedly past through the water.

Sir Lacomar's face bore a look of intense and even joyous concentration, but the stranger was looking at him oddly. "Aye, if we only had them," he said.

"Had what?" asked Barber.

"The Franconian spears; you shouted for them."

With a shock of recall, Barber realized he had said something of the kind, but before he could analyze it, Lacomar plucked at his arm.

"Look sharp now," he said, "before they get over that last bout. Which way, Cola?"

The girl pointed, and they ducked through the row of pillars around the plaza, with the leeches forming a hemisphere of foes around them. Ahead was a flight of long and wide steps that might be the entrance to an impressive building had it not been hidden by the moving swarm of leeches. Sir Lacomar led the way up, Arvicola touching him on the shoulder now and then to indicate a change of direction.

The illumination dimmed suddenly, and Barber, looking up, could see no more leeches right above. It was too high and dark within for any ceiling to be visible. Behind them, too, it was dark now, the entrance by which they had come packed with the swarming leeches, who remained behind an invisible line.

Something went Bong once with the same deliberate and decisive note that had heralded the first attack on Barber. There was a rumble; some kind of gate or movable wall slid to and cut off all sight of their pursuers. Now it was almost utterly dark, with the only light a faint bluish glow, whose source was high on a pair of cyclopean pillars. The source moved so that the light changed and threw curious shadows across their faces. "Ha!" barked the stranger-knight. "We'll make a night affair of it. Good thing there are few of us. Get in one another's way." His sword made a soughing sound as he whipped it around his head, but Lacomar said: "No, bad tactics, Acravis; dark for the attack but light for the approach," and signed to Arvicola.

She detached herself from the group and dived smoothly upward to one of the light-sources. Barber saw her fumble briefly; then light and vole together darted across to the other pillar, and in a moment she was back with a blue-glowing something in either hand.

"Take this," she said, and handed him something that squirmed so he almost dropped it. When he gripped hard its radiance brightened angrily and he could make it out as a sort of superworm, the size of a frankfurter.

"Hold it gently, Fred-froggy," she whispered, "but tight enough so it doesn't get away." She shivered with obvious nervousness.

Sir Lacomar swept out a powerful arm and drew their heads together. "You first, Acravis," he counseled, "then Cola, Barber, and I'll bring up the rear. Can get a better cut that way. Heavy metal in reserve."

Barber asked the question that had been worrying

him: "How did you two happen in at the right moment?"

Arvicola turned and touched his arm. "I—was afraid for you, so asked Sir Lacomar. . . . You're such a bloody fool, Fred."

"If we get out of this—" began Barber, and then stopped. He had intended promising to do anything she wanted, but what could a strictly temporary frog do for a water rat? If he was a temporary frog.

"Look here," Lacomar's voice rang out, suddenly loud, behind him. "Why were you afraid, my gal? This leech-Boss isn't—His Nibs, is he?"

The girl turned a stricken face. "Yes. Quiet. If he hears us, we die."

Acravis stumbled with a clank of metal and cursed in a low voice. Cola reached her light past him, and Barber caught a glimpse of a huge helical staircase, going down, down. "Let your light dim," she murmured, gripping his fingers and pulling them back gently. The worm lay quiescent; in the pale glow he could only just see the back of the girl's head before him, only just hear Lacomar coming behind, moving with surprising noiselessness for all his armored bulk.

Stairs. Barber had to feel with his toes for the edge of each next step. If it were not there, he would go tumbling . . . no, wait, underwater he did not have to fear falling whatever else betide. But something might swoop from above—and what good were all their precautions, since that entrance door had slid shut behind them? It was proof positive that whoever ruled this grim place knew of their presence . . .

The girl reached back and touched his arm again, so unseen that it made him start. Her other hand, with the worm, was pointing forward, just over Acravis' shoulder, the faint glow reflecting from the side of his helmet. Barber noted that the knight no longer stood a level below, and sure enough, at the next step, he found the stair ended. They were in a passage. Cola kept one hand on his with the lightest of touches, the other guiding Acravis, and Barber, by reaching back, could just link with Sir Lacomar in the same fashion. There was a faint, dulled clink of armor, echoed by another from the knight ahead. Then he stopped.

The girl whirled round, soundless and so suddenly that Barber was almost overbalanced, her lips against his cheek. "Won't hurt you for once, old thing," she breathed voicelessly. "We may—never—again—" and her lips sought his and clung to them for a brief, thrilling, perilous moment. There was a snorting chuckle from Lacomar behind, no louder than a snore.

Ahead, the wall was a big and solid door which moved noiselessly at Cola's light push. No light inside. The floor, soft and squeezy between Barber's toes, was obscenely like walking on something's huge tongue.

One step—two, three, four, five, six, and he lost count. Had something moved in the blackness ahead? No—yes; Acravis apparently caught it too, for he stumbled slightly, pulled back and bumped the girl, sent her caroming into Barber's left arm and shoulder. The sausagelike light worm was almost knocked from his grasp; he recovered it with a violent effort and gripped the thing hard. Its light pealed forth in that black place like the sudden blare of a pipe organ.

"No!" came Arvicola's frantic stage-whisper. "It is forbidden!" But in the flickering moment before the glow faded Barber had just time to see what it was had moved.

It was his own reflection in a big mirror; and beneath that mirror on a little shelf lay Titania's crook-handled wand.

He released the worm, which went slithering off

into the water, back and forth, and snatched for the wand. As his hand touched it, the glow from Arvicola's light just permitted him to notice what he had not seen before—some lettering, so deeply engrailed into the glass as to be part of its structure. He shoved his face close and read:

> *"On the pathway you trace*
> *The face that you face*
> *Is the median place."*

"Come—oh, quick!" said the vole's voice close in his ear; her hand gripped his wrist urgently. The thought struck him that here was another of those mysterious shrines like that in the Kobold Caverns, and he pulled loose, turned, reaching for the mirror with the tip of the wand.

A violent electric shock ran up his arm and all through him, but before he could analyze it or even think of it, there was a clank of armor. He caught the flickering reflection of Acravis' blade, heard him pant with effort once. Then he vanished. In the place where he had been, in the glow of the swimming worm, was a new, deeper darkness; a shapeless something that almost filled that side of the chamber, with two expressionless eyes that reflected.

At that same instant there came to Barber's ears a deafening gurgle of water; stinging wetness in his eyes and nostrils, crushing pressure on his chest. He saw only vaguely that Arvicola was flashing past, heard her shout, "Fred—oh, Fred!" in a voice that trailed off into an agonized scream as the blackness wrapped round her. He tried to swing the anlace, opened his mouth to shout, found it suddenly filled with water and himself strangling, choking, desperate for air; struck out frantically, and felt himself rising, up—up, toward a pinpoint of light above. The last

glimpse was of Sir Lacomar, hewing away two-handed
in the direction of those lidless eyes, and then he was
swimming.

His head broke surface. He tried to take a deep
breath and burst into a violent spasm of coughing
that brought up a pint of water before he got, at long
last, his precious gulp of air. Too weak to do more
than dog-paddle, he propelled himself feebly toward
the shore.

The bright moon of Fairyland was above, picking
out around him a little river that wound among tree-
lined banks. The scene was cousin-german to that he
had left, how long ago?—for the dive that had turned
him into a frog. He was no frog now. As a frog you
did not choke in water, you could really swim. No;
frog, man, or whatever he was, he could forget that
half-formed thought of diving back to Arvicola's
rescue. He had gone through another metamorphosis,
a shaping as these Fairylanders called it, no turning
back ever.

Something was attached to his back, hampering him
grievously. His knee bumped bottom, and he almost
sprawled, but managed to crawl the rest of the way,
dripping and surprised as he touched dry earth to find
he was still holding Titania's wand. He almost collapsed, but the thing attached to his back brought him
up and made him look over his shoulder.

The bumps that had been on his back at Oberon's
palace and had grown so astonishingly in the Kobold
Caverns had sprouted full. He had a well-developed
pair of wings, springing from the lower ends of his
shoulder blades. And the effort to stretch one of them
out for inspection told him that he also possessed the
necessary structure of bone and muscle to work them.
The effort ended in a gasp as the wings stood fully
spread and revealed.

They were bat wings.

CHAPTER XV

The wand was still clutched in his hand. For a moment or two he gazed at it, only half comprehending its import in the wave of revulsion and self-hatred that swept over him. Bat wings; that explained it. He had turned, or turned himself, into some kind of willy-nilly devil, condemned to bring evil to everyone he touched.

For that was the only possible explanation of the chain of disasters that followed his actions. If it had not been for his willful insistence on venturing to Hirudia, Arvicola might have lived out her carefree existence—and the doughty but dimwitted crawfish-knights . . . They might have come through then, but for his carelessness with the light. He thought again of the girl's appeal for help, which he had so ill answered, and for one wild moment contemplated diving into the pool again. Dead leeches were afloat on its surface, unpleasantly breaking the moonlight ripple. No; down there he would be a man again, and they crawfish and leech and vole. He had gone through the metamorphosis, another change as radical as the one that had brought him to this world. Perhaps there would be no escape from it but along the route of an endless series of such unsought adventurings. He was a god to the water-world now, and like most gods, of limited and negative powers, without capacity for helping those he liked. One could only carry on . . .

Toward disaster for the other inhabitants of this

unreasonable world. He thought of Noah Fawcett and his declining stock of iron tools; had brought the kobolds to ruin too, though they probably deserved it. Even the woodsprite, Malacea—

"I knew, I knew," said a voice. "Who dares say I cannot see tomorrow? Even beneath that great beard I knew."

Barber jumped a foot, sat down on the tails of his own wings, jumped up again to flap them and the next moment found himself scrambling and clinging among the branches overhead. That sugary accent could belong only to the girl he had just been thinking about. He looked down; sure enough, there she was, arms outstretched and gazing at him. He wrapped the wings about him, suddenly conscious of the nudity to which he had given no attention while a frog, and hunched on the limb like a gargoyle.

She trilled laughter at him, then in a breath turned serious: "I crave pardon," she said, "for forgetting that laughter makes you mortals angry. If it be within your rules of conduct to forgive the fault without penalty, I beg you, do; if not, I'll gladly bear whatever you put upon me."

A reply seemed in order. "I don't want to put anything on you," said Barber sensibly. "I want my clothes, to put on me."

Her eyes narrowed calculatingly; and she flung up one hand in a sharp gesture. "Stupid that I am to forget mortals are under no laws compelling conduct but those they impose on themselves! Yet how am I to serve you in this? I have not hid them."

"No, but—" began Barber, and stopped, embarrassed at showing embarrassment before this child of nature.

"But they're near and you'd be solitary to put them on—is that it? Poor mortal, I suppose that is your modesty, clinging like a remnant of the world you came from. Discard it; we are each other's fate, you and I, and in this land of Fairy, hiding from such fate is presumption."

She was certainly speaking the truth, but Barber hoped only the truth as she understood it. The thought of this full-bosomed and cloying wench after Cola made him shudder. "All the same, I want my clothes," he said obstinately.

She spun round, moving her hands in and out, then fixing like a pointer dog, took a dozen steps and was stooping at a clump of fern. She lifted something triumphantly—Barber could make out the flash of color that would be his clothes—but the next instant staggered back and dropped with a little shriek. "The Metal! It burns! O lovely mortal, help me!"

It would have taken an ox to be impervious to that appeal. Barber spread his wings and parachuted down beside her, pulling her away from contact with the sword which had caused the trouble. The cry was no phony on Malacea's part; a six-inch gash with singed edges showed in the filmy material of her dress, and beneath it the forearm bore a long, angry welt.

As Barber looked at it, she pushed herself up to a sitting posture and flung the other arm around his neck. "Damn it!" he said, trying to push her away. "Malacea, you're a woman of one idea."

"And that idea old. But not stale; they say the world still has a use for it.

> *"Come live with me and be my love,*
> *And we will all the pleasures prove—"*

"I might be glad to if I didn't have other business and weren't afraid your boy friend the Plum might find us together again."

"Oh, you need fear him no longer."

"I know it. I ate some of his fruit."

"He has escaped that spell. He gave your wand to some wizard of the Pool—the Base One, the Under

One, I am not sure of his name—and received an enchantment in exchange, to free him from the power of those who had eaten his fruit. I meant rather that you can handle the Metal. With that—" she pointed at the sword and he felt her shudder slightly—"at the door of my place, he can never enter. We can love nightlong and fearless."

"And in the day you'd have to go to your tree. It isn't logical."

"What does that mean? A magic word?"

"No, it means according to the laws of consistent reasoning. Things equal to the same thing are equal to each other, nothing can be both true and false, and two and two make four."

"A mortal word; and like most such, not true."

"Oh, but it is." Barber disengaged himself and picked up four pebbles, two in each hand. "Look," he said, "two!" and then opened the other hand to show the others, "Two!" He clapped the two hands together and opened them again, "Four!"

"No," said Malacea.

Barber looked and gaped. His opened hands held five pebbles.

It might have been an accident, or she might have dropped one in. He tossed away the extra stone, shut both hands resolutely, and clapped them together again.

"Now will you admit there are four?" he demanded belligerently.

"No," said Malacea. She was right. There were eight pebbles, but this time the tree sprite did not laugh.

"My love and fate," she said, laying a hand on his arm, "let me beg you, once for all, to lay aside those stiff mortal thoughts. There's no living in a country, or a world, but by its laws. There have been mortals here that could not. They wander like sad shadows till some accident pitches them back to their sty, or they turn to mere walking vegetables, like one who keeps a farm near here and whom you have doubtless seen. But this time it is more than a little important, and not me alone, though you are my very dear; for we of *the* forest can often see hidden things, and I swear by my life that of all who have ever come here you are the nearest to fulfilling the prophecy. If you but hold to the true line."

"What prophecy? And what is the true line?"

"Why, the prophecy of the redbeard that shall mean life and grace to us all! Look, you have the wand and the red beard and the power of Metal! And for the true line, that is no more than to hold straight to the task in the face of all impediments."

Barber's hand flew to his chin. He was aware that his beard had grown since his experience in the water-world, but the touch showed him how surprisingly it had spread into the great chest mattress of a nineteenth-century patriarch—and it was red, all right, the end strands showing a brick color which he never would have believed his chin capable of producing.

"But look here," he said, "haven't you just furnished me with the best possible argument against staying with you? How can I stick to the task, whatever it is, and go off with you, too?"

Her eyes suddenly stared into vacancy and her voice went to a whisper. "It's true," she said slowly, "true I might have known that to set my love on one of the great ones would be to share his hard rule of achievement before enjoyment. Go, then." She gave him a little push with the flat of her hand and Barber felt as though he had struck a child. "Go and tell your new love that Malacea the dryad sends her hate. . . . No, wait. At least you shall kiss my arm that you burned with your Metal and make it well."

She held it out and Barber obediently kissed the place where the burn was now swelling to blister. Somewhat to his surprise it immediately became as smooth—and as semitransparent—as the other arm.

He turned to his clothes with a trace of irresolution
and began to pull them on. Malacea had turned her
back to him, and did not look round even when he
was, with some difficulty, buttoning the jacket around
the bases of his wings. As he stood on tiptoe before
leaping away into flight he could see that her head
had sunk forward and her shoulders were shaken with
sobs.

With each powerful stroke his big new pectoral
muscles bulged out the front of his jacket. He cleared
the trees easily, and straightened away in level flight
across the forest through which he had toiled on foot.
Bat wings might not be pretty, but they were certainly efficient about getting one over territory. Barber
did a loop and a couple of barrel rolls just for the hell
of it, and zoomed along, savoring the pleasure of this
new physical motion, all his depression fled. So he
was near to fulfilling the prophecy of the redbeard,
was he? What prophecy? Everyone seemed to know
of it; there was that tune Malacea and then Arvicola
had sung—devilish odd, now that he thought of it,
that denizens of such different worlds should have
the same air and same words. There had been something about a redbeard, too, on that big tomb in the
graveless graveyard, the one that bore the same
strange heraldic design as the door in the Kobold
Caverns.

It all tied together somehow and somewhere. Barber
experienced the maddening sense that comes just before the climax of a good detective story, of having all
the clues laid out before him, but being unable to in-
terpret them into a meaningful pattern. Or did he
have all the clues? There seemed one missing from
the set; he ought to be doing something, having some
authority he did not now possess. The accomplish-
ment of whatever he had to do waited on that; even
if what he had to do was only to get back where he
belonged through one more of these insane permuta-

tions. Perhaps the clues never would make sense in this impossible cosmos. He thought of the pebbles, and clapping his wings behind his back in irritation, did a fifteen-foot drop.

Long black striding shadows beneath hinted of moonset, and he guessed it must be near dawn till he remembered Malacea's counsel to forget his imported habits of thought. But what time was it, then? —or since time appeared a matter of no consequence, which way lay Oberon's palace? He flapped and soared easily—the motion was no more difficult than walking—while he considered the question. A thin haze of cirrus diluted the moonlight above him; neither Fawcett's farm nor the Kobold Hills were visible.

But wasn't there something moving up there to his right? He spiraled toward it.

As he approached the vision resolved itself into a small female sprite sailing nonchalantly along on gauzy wings.

"Beg pardon," Barber called up, "could you—"

"Why, 'tis the King's new changeling!" she cried. "And alate—not to mention barbed like a centaur. Well met! What's toward?"

"Why, I'd like to find my way to the palace."

"There to cozen more fays with unmeant gambits in the game of love, I'll be bound." She laughed at him and did a couple of butterfly flip-flops.

"No. . . . Say, aren't you the girl who was in Oberon's apartment when Titania came home?"

"Nay, not I; 'twas no more than one of our band— Idalia. But an you think to hold matters secret in Fairyland, Sir Changeling, let me undeceive you. The very trees are sib to all that stirs. How else would I know that you're but newly come from the embrace of the apple sprite, Malacea?"

Barber wondered if his flush was visible in the moonlight and on the wing. "I assure you, I—"

"Come sir, no hoity-toity manners; the whole mat-

ter's exposed. The world knows that your conscience
is clear enough—which swinish commodity you seem
to value highly, being mortal—but I cannot say as
much for your courtesy."

"But look here, do you mean to tell me that everyone knows everything that happens to everyone else?"

"To be sure, witling, in so far as they are interested enough to discover."

"Then Queen Titania knew all the time that
Oberon had this Idalia at the palace?"

"She were marvelously less than the Queen's Resplendency did she not."

"Then why didn't she make a fuss when she came
in? And why was it necessary for me to get Idalia out
of there so fast? Sounds like Dinkelspiel to me."

"Soft, soft, you'd choke the goose to death to make
him cough eggs from 's crop. Why, as to take your
first question first, since it holds the nub of the mat-
er—because she could not; the laws of conduct forbade,
there being no trace of Cousin Idalia within the
apartment."

"Oh." Barber digested that for a moment, flying
along beside her, and reflecting that he had heard
something of the same kind before. "Very convenient
laws. Who makes them?"

The fay went off into a long peal of laughter,
curiously soft in the unechoing sky. "Makes 'em? Why,
child, they're laws natural and were made with the
world. . . . Stay, I do forget you're of mortal kindred,
who live by other rules. Tell me, is it good fact, as
some say, that in the land you come from all the dumb
world follows an immutable procession, as the sun
arriving punctually on hour or the seed producing
nought but the tree that bore it?"

"Why, certainly."

"Even so the laws of conduct. When I laughed but
now had you laughed with me, we must have spent
half the night tumbling and playing awing through

these light airs. For we be wingèd, you and I; have too much in us of the light elements, Fire and Air, to be restrained from joy by the troubles of the earth-bound court."

"What's wrong with the court?"

"What's not? The worst and heaviest of the shapings; all's confusion, and the King's Radiance fears some deadly doom. And so, farewell; I'm for a new master."

"Wait a second!" cried Barber. "I'd like to get to the palace, and I'd like still more to see you again. How do I go about it?"

"Ask the wind—or your Malacea." And off she went, at a speed he could not match.

CHAPTER XVI

Which direction he should take was left pretty much in the air, Barber thought, wishing there were someone around to appreciate the pun. If the fay were bound away from the court it would not do to follow her; and from what he had learned of the singular geography of Fairyland, it seemed probable that if he followed her back track he would reach some very interesting place, but not the one he was looking for. The thing to do was think in terms of his environment—"lay aside those stiff mortal thoughts" as Malacea had advised. What would a Fairylander do?

Use the wand, he answered himself, letting it slide from his hand. It fell, not straight down but sliding and twisting down an invisible gradient like a falling leaf, as though trying to hold itself in one direction. Barber did a power dive in time to catch it before it reached the treetops and slanted up again, holding the loop of the wand loosely in a crooked forefinger. "All right," he ordered it, "suppose you show me the way."

The wand thrust itself out, flatly horizontal, and Barber flew along in the direction it indicated. Beneath him the forest began to thin out into clumps and groves, then altogether wore away into a rolling plain, with only a tree here and there, black in the waxing light. Now outcroppings of rock began to jut through the grass of the plain, growing in size and frequency till Barber found himself flying low over a rugged crag country, which presently sprang up in

peaks as angular as the mountains of the moon. Not
a sign of the smooth parkland and monstrous potted
trees that he remembered.

Off ahead the sky was lightening. The country below, now all gorge and precipice, threw up a tor that
stood with scarred sides across his line of flight. On its
top, black against the Prussian-blue gloom that pre-
cedes sunrise, something good, too regular in outline to be the work of nature. A castle—ugly and
squat in contour, with thick unpierced curtain walls
and disproportionately small towers at the angles,
like a prison. A Dracula castle—no, that would have
the fascination of the weird, something Gothic out of
Aubrey Beardsley, while this was as hideous as a
factory town. The wand led him straight to it, and as
he planed in for a landing at the gate he saw Oberon's
blue-and-gold oriflamme hanging listlessly from a staff.

The gate was heavy wood, bound with metal in a
finicking and tasteless design. It was locked; there was
no answer to either Barber's shout or his hammerings,
but when he thought of the wand again and applied
it, the gate creaked grudgingly just wide enough to let
him enter. He found himself in a courtyard with a
little dry grass sticking up through cobbles, and the
first thing he noticed was the slobbering hobgoblin
with overlarge knee joints who had admitted him. The
second was Oberon, Titania and Gosh, coming down
the steps of the donjon.

As they crossed the bailey Barber had full time to
note that, if he had changed his journey, there was
still more pronounced a change in them, and all for
the worse. Oberon looked older and balder, with a
hunched and gnarled appearance hard to put a name
to; one of those things you were sure you saw till you
looked straight at it, when it vanished. Titania's pale
glory of complexion had become a dead white, the
ruffles at her neck were a little askew and the gold
broidery of her sleeves tarnished. The good-natured

impishness of Gosh's face had given way to a fixed
malignant sneer, as though he could not wait to grow
up into a ruffian and a killer.

And as with master, so with man. The train that
followed the royal pair was an assemblage of crapu-
lous horrors, not a winged fairy in the crew. Some
limped, some had gargantuan hands or chins, some
tails, and all deformities. Barber recognized Imponens
with difficulty; the acrobatic philosopher was hobbling
along on a cane, with the corners of his mouth drawn
down, and only just lifted his foot out of the way as a
huge centipede scuttled from under the feet of another of the crew.

The King stretched out his neck and scrooged up
his eyes, peering at Barber as though he could not see
well. "No, tell me not," he said. "Memory's as good
as ever, a faculty independent of mutations, which
does not decay. Ha, I have it—you're the latest changeling, Barber."

"Just back from the Kobold Hills, at your service,
and reporting complete success." He managed a salute
with the wand. Around the King the court burst into
squeaks and murmurs and Oberon almost smiled.

"Well done, then; you have our favor. Success were
needed at this pass, sorely needed. Even a tiny gobbet
goes far to restore our joy."

"Joy is but the absence of pain," croaked Imponens, but Barber had already begun with: "Is this your
new palace?"

"Aye," said Oberon, "though we had not the plan-
ning of't. Come, we'll change tales and wring each
other's vitals—" He reached out to take Barber's arm
and lead him toward the frowning keep, then drew
back. "You have the Metal about you. Leave it by
the gate, my lord Barber; 'twill at least be some barrier
to the bugs and bewitchings that now do plague us."

Barber put his sword just inside the gate as directed
and followed the King. The "my lord" was a new form

of address but jangled a pleasantly responsive chord somewhere in his mind. Within the castle their footsteps went echoing through great passages of undressed stone, taller than those of the Kobold Caverns, but almost as dank. There were spiderwebs everywhere, and less pleasant insects crawling about. When they came to a great hall whose walls bore faded and moldering tapestries, Oberon dismissed the court with a word and led on, up a circular stone staircase to the battlements. The dawnlight was growing and a chill wind had come up with it, that wrenched at their bodies as Barber told his story.

"So she saw in you the destined redbeard," said Oberon, when he had finished." 'Tis a thing to think on; must ask Imponens, whose counsel in such affairs is never less than good, though somewhat vinegar'd with pessimism of late. Yet it could be, and being solve the sorrows of—"

Something hit Barber violently in the back, tumbling him right through one of the crenels in the battlement. He had one glimpse of young Gosh's snarling face, heard Oberon's startled shout, and the wind whistled past as the toothlike rocks below swam up to receive him.

There was a heart-stopping instant of terror before Barber remembered and spread his wings. They bore; he leveled out in a long sweeping catenary, and beat his way back to the parapet. Oberon was trying to get at the boy, who was wrapping himself in Titania's skirts for protection. Barber made a quick estimate of speed, distance and windage, fluttered his wings twice for altitude, and glided in.

Gosh saw him coming, and left his hiding place to run, but Barber swooped in, swinging the wand with both hands like a bat, to bring it across the boy's shoulders. If it broke every bone in the young imp's body he would be only too pleased.

The wand met only the slightest resistance. Then

Gosh was not there, and Barber, thrown off balance
by the strength of his own blow, swept into a stum-
bling landing.

"Whither went he?" cried Titania. "You villain,
you puling thrip, if you've destroyed him, I'll—"

"You'll do precisely nothing, madam," Oberon cut
in. "An he were destroyed, 'twere a bad world rid
of worse rubbish, but 'tis not so. There he stands, by
power of the wand and 's own character given his
proper form at last."

He pointed to the battlement beside Titania, and
the others, turning, saw a crocodile about a foot and
a half long, which opened its jaws to emit a faint
sound like "Urk!" and started across the paving at a
brisk clockworky waddle.

Titania snatched up the reptile. "Poor Chandra!"
she said, contriving in some odd manner to be both
pathetic and ridiculous without in the least losing her
character of queenliness. "Oh, I could smile to see
them die that bring these shapings on us." She cod-
dled the thing in her arms like a baby and Barber
was surprised to see two big tears oozing from its
eyes along its scaly face. "I—" began Titania, when
the memory of a legend clicked in Barber's brain. Absurd where he came from, it was probably true here.
"Drop it, quick!" he shouted, "it's going to bite!"

Titania did not quite drop the animal, but as she
half jerked it away its teeth met with a snap, half an
inch from her nose. "Gramercy for your warning,
philosophic Barber," she said.

Barber bowed: "If I may offer a suggestion to
Your Resplendency, you can keep your little playmate
very comfortable till he gets his shape back by putting
him in a pan with water and a rock he can crawl out
on. Your Resplendency can feed him once or twice a
week on chopped raw meat."

Titania gazed at him suspiciously for a moment,
then, "I'll do it, straight," she said, and hurried for

the stairs, holding her pet at arm's length, with its legs revolving. Oberon chuckled; Barber somehow could not find her distress very funny.

But the King was plucking him by the sleeve. "We've matters of state to confer on," he said. "Harkee, my lord Barber, I do count you a true man."

"I hope—"

"Tush, take it not amiss; we're surrounded by treacheries in these evil times. Why, the very cocking-wenches play at Judas— Hold, where were we? I have't; these villain shapings—secret of statecraft is let nought distract . . ." His voice trailed off and he paced the paving, hands behind back, wagging his head to and fro, then turned suddenly and gripped Barber hard by both elbows.

"I'm in some sort an usurper," he declared fiercely. "Make the worst of it; say I seized the throne and the lady. She loved me true and I her; we mutually do still, I swear it. Will you hold me the less for that?"

"Why, no, of course not," said Barber, mystified, but supposing this was what he ought to reply.

"Well then, what would you? My lady's gay and lives for pleasure in herself and those about her. Under her regiment we had a realm here like your own mortal world in its laws physical, save for slight changes such as lacking the power of iron . . . Look how yon bat sails widdershins around that tower— another presage of disaster!" He flung out an arm to point, then turned to Barber again:

"So it was all gaiety, high pleasure and good converse at court, but beyond it, misery—rievings, slayings and black magic, hideous things done, as you have traces of among your own people. Is't not so, you've heard some tale how they met on a mountain with bloody rites?"

"Like voodoo at the Walpurgis Night?"

"Aye: and they're good history of the black days ere I wedded Titania and 'stablished a new sovranty.

But these anarchies and nightmares, I put them down
with the strong arm—I. With the aid of Sylvester and
the giving of my heart's best blood I made a great
conjuring that may not be repeated; set the laws fundamental of this realm so that happiness should be our
constant companion. 'Twas not enough; there are
those whose only happiness lies in their own aggran-
dizement."

He stopped and looked out across the waste of
rock. The sun had reached the horizon now and was
throwing level ruddy beams across pillar and buttress
and spire, but it drew no answering fire from those
heartless cold pitches of frozen lava. They lay inert,
high lights and shadows alike gray and deadly. Barber cleared his throat. "Do you mean those laws of
conduct I've heard about? I wish—"

"Aye. Conduct. There's the key—would you not
say? Sylvester and I, we sublimated in a manner the
laws natural to these others, so that none could give
joy, for example, without receiving it in turn—set
a rein on all furious passions . . . Mistake . . ." He
turned and gripped Barber by the arm again. "Good
Barber, will you make alliance with an old man and
old king whose web is near spun?"

"What, me? Why? I thought I was working for you,
sir. What—"

"So, let it slip." Oberon passed a hand across his
forehead as though to brush something away. "I had
not meant to ask you so early. Let it slip; my mind
is all adossed. We'll to bed and treat with Imponens
present, who can see deeper into a millstone than
most."

He led the way to the stairs and whistled for a
servant. The one who came had the big head and pop
eyes of an idiot and teeth that hung over his lower
lip. He breathed with his mouth, blowing little
bubbles.

The room to which this creature led Barber was

tall, but narrow, with a single high window and rusty damp-streaks down the walls. The bed was hard, and Barber, who had never tried to sleep in wings before, found such difficulty in arranging his limbs that he had no more than closed eyes when he was awakened by a strident "Krawk!" and looked up to see a big black bird on the window sill with moonbeams streaming past it. Somewhere below in the castle a bell was tolling with muffled, slow persistence.

Barber's head ached and his mouth held a taste like the hangover from a three-day drunk, but there seemed little use in trying to sleep any more, as both bird and bell kept up their noise. He dressed in a foul mood; "Krawk!" said the bird as he handled each garment, cocking its head and inspecting him with embarrassing thoroughness. He thought of flying up and shooing it away, but the room was hardly wide enough for the spread of his wings, so he compromised by yelling "Beat it!" and went down to the hall.

Oberon and Titania were seated at breakfast as in that other hall, but there were no winged fairies visible and the correct frog footmen had disappeared. Instead there was a throng of the exaggerated people he had seen the night before; they stumbled over one another trying to serve the King and Queen, and the bell in the background donged steadily. The King looked up at Barber's entrance.

"A chair of pretense, ho! for Barber!" he called, and motioned to a place by his right at the table. It was forthcoming after a little commotion and Barber sat down to breakfast whose flavor was not improved by the sight of a pair of cockroaches holding a conference in the center of the table. Oberon waited courteously enough till he pushed away his plate.

"Now let's to business," said the King. "Here be deep matters. A weird lies on us—implacable, no escape within our—" his eye caught the cockroaches—"within our—faugh! what foulness! Imponens, unriddle this matter of our good cousin, Barber. What is't we wish to say?"

"Doubtless that we gave ourselves to delight while the Enemy to strivings, Your Radiance. But 'twill not mend a broken bone to see where it's fractured."

"Pox on your counsel of despair. Are we dogs to lick in gratitude the punishing hand? No: we're as foul as those that challenge this fair land an we not challenge them in turn."

"But, Your Radiance, we lack the power—" Imponens began to protest, but Oberon cut him short:

"And have we not here one that possesses all means needful? Our Barber, our war-duke and champion, who'll not be bound by—"

Titania cleared her throat. "My Lord," she said, "you do but rant and wander from the purpose. Look, Barber, here's what he would say, these witcheries my Lord King put down when he were united, they have made a great resurgence."

Barber managed to get a word in edgewise. "Will you pardon me if I say I don't understand? Whom are you talking about? Who's responsible for these troubles?"

There was a silence. Titania and Oberon looked at each other, and it was the brownie philosopher who finally spoke: "You pose, Sir Barber, the question of the ages, one ineluctable. For if I answer in detail: the kobolds, then you are well answered, since those cattle did grievously vex this realm in ancient days, and you yourself are but come from hindering a new vexation. Yet, 'twill not be the kobolds, neither; for their two excursions are separated by so wide a gap as memory can barely bridge, and in that interval they have been the best of subjects and citizens, cheerful, apt to every task, and I make no doubt will be again, now that you have knocked down their high pretensions.

"Shall I say the fays, then, for deserting the court?

Nay; they're lighthearted aerial creatures who give and receive pleasure, will be a joy wherever the laws of Oberon run.

"Those who bring these shapings on us? At the moment, my art tells me it may be those Princes of the Ice which erst were our good friends and well-wishers. Yet if they be destroyed their ambition will but pass to other hands and in the end be unconquerable. What boots it, then, to struggle—"

Titania rapped sharply on the table with her knife. "I'll not hear such traitorous doctrine!" she cried. "Give him no thought, Barber; we live in today and not i'the ages, whereas 'tis every philosopher's maggot to imagine himself thinking for eternity. Here's the present problem: someone, it may be those Princes of the Ice our lick-pudding counselor thinks, has found the gap in the laws that guard this land. By constitution its physical forms are somewhat unstable; well then, these enemies who seek to rule raise spells to produce shapings and still more, till our whole surrounding is gone hideous. Our joy fled with the fays who cannot bear such ugliness; they hope to cramp us and drive us with unpalatable circumstance till we even break our own laws of conduct, the reign slip from our hands, which they hope to seize."

"And what if they did?"

"Our death, perhaps; but in any case the tempestuous anarch disorder which my very dear Lord and King saved us from so long gone. This is what you must keep us from now, good Barber."

Fred Barber sat back in his chair of pretense and looked from King to Queen. The picture was becoming clearer, but:

"Why must it be me? What's the matter with Oberon?"

"My own curst laws!" The King brought his fist down on the table. "They hold for all—no violences.

Do I break 'em, I've let in the forbidden thing, we have the old days back. Yet here's a scoundrelism will hear no argument but sharps."

"I may be awfully dense, but again, why pick on me?"

"Why, you're the redbeard! You come of a hard race, have the iron I left out of my laws; must do it in any case, and why not the sooner." He sang, to the same tune Malacea and Cola had used:

> *"When the redbeard comes again,*
> *Then shall fairies turn to men.*
> *When he touches the three places*
> *He shall know them by their faces."*

As Oberon chanted the absurd verse, a sense of excitement invaded Barber. Once more he seemed on the edge of something he could not quite grasp, but now it was something splendid and promising as the discovery of a new world. Almost without realizing what he was doing, he stood up and clapped the great wings together behind his back. All the people in the hall gave a shout; Oberon and Titania stood up too, and the King extended his hand:

"Go, then, Barber. You are our stay and alliance as iron must cover and protect gold, however precious and desirable the latter be."

CHAPTER XVII

Go. Yes, but where?

The exaltation lasted till he had reached the castle gate, picked up his sword, and was winging out across the sea of rock through clear moonlight. He had not thought of asking directions, and it occurred to him that it would have done no good to ask. The people of the court would have answered quite honestly that they did not know. It was useless to expect from them precision in any physical or material statement.

Which way?

He had begun by flying round the castle in an Archimedian spiral, ever widening. Beneath, the tumbled rocks gave no sign of life, nothing that might be a guide. Even the distant horizon failed to show that gradation where the mountain country broke down to the craggy moors over which he had sailed the previous evening. For all he knew he might be flying straight back into Yorkshire and an aerial encounter with a Messerschmitt 109. He debated mentally whether a return to his own world under such circumstances would be more or less pleasant than continuing in this madhouse Fairyland, but could reach no decision. He reflected that this would have sent him into something like a panic a week before; now it merely afforded some faint amusement as he sailed along on tireless wings, now and again experimenting with the subtle pleasure of gliding.

It must have taken three or four hours of this kind

of flight to bring him to the gorge where he saw the
first tree, a scrawny conifer, clinging to the wall of a
glen. He circled the place two or three times, taking
bearings, before sweeping on around the now-wide
circuit. Nothing but rock was visible at any other
point, but when he returned to the region of the tree
he perceived that the glen had deepened to a cleft
between walls of stone, with a bright sliver of stream
running down it, and there were more trees.

This might repay investigation. He drove along
down the stream, which for some time showed no
disposition to widen, but rather dropped deeper till it
was running through a canyon between walls that
held scrubby plants in addition to the trees at the
bottom. But after maybe half an hour's flight more
the rock walls suddenly closed in from right and left;
the stream, pinched to a thread, burst through a narrow gate, and with a clamor audible even at his altitude, plunged down a long waterfall into a deep bowl
of a valley.

The sides were precipices save at the far lower end,
where the stream escaped again, boiling through broken boulders past walls that slanted toward the crests
to reveal a glimpse of something green beyond. The
valley itself was maybe a mile across, all trees around
the base of the rocks, all trees along the bank of the
stream, but in between lush meadow. In the center of
the meadow on the right bank a snow-white unicorn
was grazing.

Barber slanted in for a nearer look. Indubitable
unicorn. But as he came down on soundless wing, the
moon-shadow of his passing flickered across the grass.
The creature lifted its head, neighed piercingly, and
flung itself toward the trees along the river at a head-
long gallop. At the same moment Barber, hovering
low, caught another faint sound, regular-irregular, like
the unicorn's hoofbeats. *Tap, tap, tappty-tap, tap.*

Any life was welcome and information after the

blank thus far. He flipped his wings and dropped lightly to a tiptoe landing on grass as gracious as a lawn. Back under the shelter of the trees a shaft of yellow light reached upward, startling in its contrast to the blue moonglow. Barber stepped toward it cautiously, wand in left hand, the other ready to grip his sword. *Tap—tap—toc.*

The light was coming from a hole at the roots of an age-old tree. He got a glimpse of a small bearded face surmounted by a green stovepipe hat with a feather in it. At the same moment the face got a glimpse of him; there was a dull wooden slam and the spot of light vanished.

Barber stepped close to look at the base of the tree, feeling around the spot where the light had been. His fingers encountered a crevice, regular in outline—a door, made to look like part of the roots.

He rapped. The door gave a dull sound of solidity but no result, nor was there any response when he tried tapping it with the wand. But he was determined now to have converse with whatever denizen of the valley lived within, so sat down and waited patiently.

With the faintest creak the door opened a little and the light crept cautiously out. Behind it the brown, bearded face appeared.

"Hello," said Barber.

"Hello yoursel'," said the face. "Ye gave me a fright. Sure, I thought ye were someone else."

"My name's Barber. Who did you think I was?"

"A felly I know." The elf fished around behind him, brought up a shoe and began working on it, sitting on his doorsill. He spoke out of the left side of his mouth, the right side being full of pegs: "Where would ye be goin' with that fine stick an' all?"

"I'm not quite sure. To the Princes of the Ice, I think. Could you tell me which way they are?"

The elf jerked a thumb toward the outlet of the

valley. "That way. Ye'll be wan of Oberon's folk.
The back o' me hand to ye, thin. If I'd known that—
annyway, I'm hopin' the ice people bate the livin'
bedad out o' ye."

"Very courteous of you," remarked Barber drily.
"You're on their side?"

"Not at all, at all. I'm hopin' that in the ind ye
bate the princes, for 'tis mane divils they are. But I'm
hopin' they give ye a good taste o' the stick first."

"Why?"

"That's to pay ye out for what Huon did to us."

"And what did this Huon do to you?"

"Mane to say ye don't know? A great Barney's bull
o' a scandal, that was. Oberon would have the idee
o' civilizin' us, he called it, and sint Sir Huon to do
his dirty work. Oh, that was the disthressful time, with
batin's and evictions and turnin' us into frogs. Me
own brother Usnech, the darlin', was wan o' those
turned."

"My word, I didn't know Oberon went in for that
sort of thing. When did this happen?"

"Wan thousand, six hundred, and eighty-four years
ago, three months and sivin days to the minute."

"That seems like a long time to carry a grudge. You
certainly keep track of it."

The elf wagged his head stubbornly. "Murther's
murther, and oppression's oppression, whether 'twas
tin thousand years ago or yesterday. And all because
the boys would be havin' their fun. Oh 'twas cruel;
as though we'd forget and be friends."

"Well, why not after all this time? Didn't he make
things better all around?"

"And what does that matter whin the heart is dead
within ye? Be off with you, mortal, and tell that royal
rogue he'll get no help from the luchrupáns." The elf
drove the last peg into the shoe with a vicious whack,
dropped back in his hole and slammed the door.

It occurred to Barber that he had not asked for

help, but there was no use mentioning this to a closed door. He was just getting up to go when he saw what he had not noticed before—that a climbing rose wound round the base of the tree, embracing it so closely that there was barely room for the mannikin's door to open. Though it was full night the vine bravely lifted bud and open flower to the sky, rich double blooms with petals of mingled white and red, with an almost piercing fragrance. Barber bent to admire one; a vagrant air from nowhere bent the branch ever so slightly toward him as though to invite plucking.

> *"Röslein, Röslein, Röslein rot,*
> *Röslein auf der Heiden . . ."*

he murmured as he set it in his buttonhole, ran a few steps across the green lawn to gain momentum for the start and was just about to take off when a tiny shaft of light shot from the reopened door, a voice called "Up the ice!" and there was a crisp wooden slam. Barber laughed as he rode upward, spiraling out of the encircling cliffs. There was no further sign of the unicorn; but now as he drove toward the valley outlet movement again showed between him and the moon.

Company of any kind were welcome, but as long wingbeats carried him toward this company he perceived it was not human but avian—the same big black bird that had looked at him across the window sill that morning, or its twin brother. It stretched its neck under a wing to regard him as he approached and remarked "Krawk!" in a friendly manner.

"Hello, birdie," said Barber. "Would you be a raven? You look pretty well grown."

"Krawk!" said the bird again, did a marvelous inside loop and fell in beside him. It was evidently as fond of companionship as Barber himself.

Below, the stream had broken from its valley prison

and was flowing through a wide canyon with a rumble
of rapids. The mountains were still wild and rugged,
but not quite so harsh or waterless, slashed here and
there with high gullies which evidently held springs,
for trees grew along them, closing in farther down to
mantle all the lower slopes. Barber eased downward to
look for further signs of life. There were none; and
he was just turning back to glide up a long hill-
current when a wild shriek from the raven caught his
ear.

He half turned; the motion saved him, for at that
moment something big and black dropped on him
from above, and but for that warning would have
caught him between the shoulders. As it was, a violent
blow carried him down toward the treetops, something long and sharp and deadly dug through the back
side of his trunks and came out with a rending of cloth
as Barber put his full power into his wingbeat.

He banked, fumbling for the kobold sword, and
trying to bring the attacker into vision. A hiss of
feathers overhead accompanied by a second cry from
the raven gave him momentary warning again, and
he put strength into a drive forward and up. The
change of pace threw his attacker more wildly off, but
something slashed down a calf muscle. As he felt his
hose turn warm with blood another bank gave him
a view of these attackers, now below and beating up
toward him.

They were giant black eagles, almost as big as he
was, and a second glance showed him that each had
two (2) well-developed heads. One of them was, in
fact, snapping and striking with one head at the raven
which swooped over it, while the other head spied
for direction. But it was only a glimpse; the warning
hiss sounded again and Barber jerked frantically sidewise to dodge the strike of a third eagle. The tip of a
black wing caught him a dizzying blow on the side of
the head, knocking off his plumed hat.

He made a quick estimate of the distance between himself and the rocks, then threw himself on his back to see where these heraldic monstrosities were coming from. At first he could make out nothing; then he spotted two more, almost exactly between him and the moon. One was diving, close enough to grow visibly in size as he watched, but not diving at him, for beneath the stroke Barber saw moon-reflection from the glossy back of another raven. The bird avoided; there was a flurry of motion as the eagle checked and the two ramped against each other, their battle cries thinned by distance. Then the second eagle folded its wings and came in on Barber.

Two could play at that game, he thought, flipping over into normal flying position and dropping for the mountain crests. Wind whistled through his hair in ascending pitch. Behind he heard a high, piercing screech, the sound of a rusty hinge. It had a distinct warble; no doubt, thought Barber, the heterodyning effect of a slight difference in pitch between the two larynxes belonging to a single eagle.

The top of a mountain grew at him, jagged and formidable. He spread and leveled off, with the strain tearing at his pectoral muscles. The horrible thought came to him that he'd miscalculated, he'd crash, didn't have strength to pull out of the dive . . .

Then the mountaintop drove past. He was still going down, but down a slope, and a twig-tip slashed across the back of his right hand. At his hundred-mile-an-hour speed it stung like a whip and left a little line of emergent blooddrops.

A glance showed that the eagle above had pulled up sooner than himself and was now joined by one of those that had attacked at first. Far off, another was engaged with one of the friendly ravens and seemed to be winning, for the smaller bird was only trying to beat off the attack and get away. Before he could make up his mind to do anything about it the two eagles above became three—five—six, they tipped over and came plummeting down at him with nerve-shattering screams.

Barber, cocking his head this way and that, dodged like the bat whose wings he bore. A claw touched his cheek. He tacked frantically; a wing struck one of his own, half numbing it and sending him tumbling. As he forced the painful member to pump, a victory-scream sounded from behind, probably over one of the ravens, he thought angrily, and put on speed.

The eagles had shot past, low over the valley. Now they swirled up in a cloud and sorted themselves into a diagonal line, like geese. Three more swam up out of nowhere and attached themselves to the end of the line, and they came toward him, all nine pairs of wings flapping in synchronism. Their intention was obvious. With a jar Barber realized that those predatory double-headers held brains enough for intelligent combination. One or two he could dodge, but nine, diving in quick succession, would get him sure.

He flew at utmost speed for a few moments, then came round in a sweeping circle to see whether they would follow if he affected to give up the direction he had chosen. They did; the hostility was implacable then, related to his existence and not his movements. There was nothing to do but fight them then, and oddly remembering a quotation from Kipling to the effect that a savage attacked was much less dangerous than a savage attacking, he pivoted on easy wings and slanted upward, whipping out the sword.

The eagle formation—another had joined it now—came up with him, holding the same strict alignment, but with the birds craning their doubled necks and screeching at each other, as though in perplexity. Barber felt a momentary thrill of gratification. He hoped it was not wishful thinking to deduce that, although the monsters were capable of plan, they lacked mental flexibility, the capacity to meet an unforeseen situation. He could climb faster, too, with his wide wing-spread and better balance; he was past and gaining, the formation went a little uncertain, and he peeled off into an almost vertical drop.

The sword-arm came down with the added motion of his descent, taking one of them where wing joined body, and Barber shouted with delight as he felt the blade bite through. The eagle went spinning and screeching downward; Barber gave one swift wing-stroke and brought his sword up backhand onto the neck of the next in line. One head flew from the body, the other head squeaked, and the eagle began to fly in a zany circle. Another swing sent one tumbling in a tangle of feathers, and the formation broke up, eagles spreading in all directions.

Barber pursued one, caught it and killed it with a blow. Kipling was right and the things were practically helpless against attack from above. He went into a long glide to gain distance, looking for, but see-ing no sign of the ravens. They must have been fin-ished off, poor birds. Off in the distance the formation he had broken up was gathering again, and more eagles were coming up, some to reinforce the shattered group, others to form a new one, which immediately began to climb.

Barber drove for altitude, got above them, and dived in, killing several eagles. But the other forma-tion climbed while he was about it and delivered a diving attack; it took both sharp flying and quick swordwork to get away unscathed. While he was about it more eagles came up to join those already on hand; there must be at least twenty-five or thirty not count-ing those he had got rid of. At this rate they would smother him with mere press of numbers long before the night was done, and he had no assurance that the confounded double-headers were not diurnal.

Clearly, this counterattack in the air would get him nowhere in the long run, and equally clearly something better would have to be found soon. The eagles, he observed, climbing to stay above the latest arrivals, all seemed to come from the same direction. Probably they belonged to the forces of that mysterious Enemy to whom Oberon had referred. Their sudden attack might be on general principles, due to original sin, but the way they had kept after him even when he turned back did not look like it. Neither did their constant multiplication. More likely he was getting too close for comfort to that third place of the Fairyland prophecy.

Too close for the Enemy's comfort. He recalled how his touch on the first of those places had put a stop to the kobolds' antisocial activities and wondered whether there had been any improvement in the tangled and difficult life of the Pool since he touched the second. Below him forty-five or fifty double-headed eagles were circling and screaming, spreading to form a network which should be too wide and deep for penetration. He was so high now that the mountains beneath had lost relief and were spread like a flat picture map, with shadows and patches of green for coloring.

If he took the bull by the horns and sought out the birds' point of origin, he might both find the third place and cut off the supply of eagles at its source. In any event, it seemed the only plan worth trying, since going back to Oberon with this following of impossible eagles did not commend itself.

Other eagles were coming to join those beneath him, their direction clearly marked from this height. He swooped down a thousand feet or so, and saw the latest comers circle round to join those gathering in a cloud of wings behind him. In addition to the ability to combine efforts, they evidently possessed a good communications system and had passed on word that he was too dangerous an opponent for singlehanded attack.

After a while no more eagles seemed to be coming. Barber circled, looking down, and perceived that he was over an amazingly tall, prominent peak. His eyesight seemed exceptionally good—probably another Fairyland gift, like the wings. Another circle; behind, the eagles were spreading out in a widening crescent to shut him in, methodically and with no indication of haste. A single eagle came soaring up from the shadow of the peak; Barber closed wings, dove and killed it before it knew he was there, noticing as he did so that the shadow from which it had flown held a single spot of iridescent light.

Toward this he flew; as he did so, the flock behind him burst into screams and began to close, overhead as well as on all sides. But he held course and came to a landing on the ledge where the spot was.

It was a ball of some brownish but shiny substance, perhaps a yard in diameter. Barber tapped it with his sword and was instantly rewarded by a chorus of screams from the eagles above. The ball gave off a sharp, dry wooden sound, and when he swung at it full arm, only moved slightly without breaking. It appeared to be attached to the ledge.

The eagles overhead screamed again and one swooped at Barber. He struck it down, a neat blow, right between the paired necks. Another dove at him, and as he dodged, crashed into the rocks and went tumbling a thousand feet down in a cloud of feathers.

A sharp *ping* made Barber look round. The globe had vanished into a haze of golden particles. On the ledge where it had been sat a new young eagle, shaking dampness from its feathers. It spied Barber and opened its beaks, but he took both heads off with a single sweeping stroke, and dodged another suicidal dash from above.

On the spot where ball and then eagle had been was a circular hole in the ledge, about the size of a broomstick, with a smooth, shiny lip. As Barber watched, with glances overhead, another sphere appeared at the mouth of this hole and grew like a bubble.

Two more eagles had died in attacks from above when this one reached the size of the first. Barber twice hit it with all his strength and no result. A moment later it shattered. Barber killed the eagle it contained and kicked its carcass off the ledge; a proceeding obviously futile, since a new egg began to grow immediately. The process appeared endless, and there was nothing to plug the hole with, the ledge as bare as a banker's head and as hard as his heart.

Another eagle swooped from above, and as Barber lowered his sword after cutting down the bird his elbow touched Titania's wand, still stuck through his belt. The very thing! When the next egg dissolved, he rapidly slew the eagle it contained, reached over and before the new bubble could come forth, rammed the wand in. It went home to a tight fit, and from within the hole came a bubbling tumult like the cooking of a gigantic kettle, but no more balls appeared.

The eagles above burst into such an ear-splitting racket that Barber could hardly hear himself think, and all around him began diving at the cliff in witless frenzy. Thump! Thump! they landed, bounding off into the black depths below with flying feathers, utterly neglecting Barber in their furious desire for death; and soon there were no more eagles visible, on the ledge or in the sky. The tubelike orifice still gave forth a sound of boiling. Barber did not quite dare to withdraw the wand, but after a few minutes' rest, he hung his sword at his side and took to wing again.

As he soared above the peak in now-empty air he noted something unseen before on the far horizon. Not a mountain nor a meadow, it was as tall as the former and wide as the latter, smooth and shining like the roc's egg of Sindbad. Barber flew toward it.

CHAPTER XVIII

Ice. The roc's egg was ice.

Fred Barber knew it long before he arrived at that glistening and translucent structure by the chill that hung round it, though that chill—strangely, to his senses attuned to another world—brought no mist in the air and the great dome showed no sign of melting. "Princes of the Ice," Oberon had said, and this was doubtless their residence, the central seat of power of that Enemy he was arrayed against.

Locked in the heart of the icy dome, distorted by curvature and refraction, was something dark and shapeless. Barber lit near it and shivered for the first time in Fairyland in the constant current of cold air flowing outward. Whatever lay at the heart of that gelid bubble remained ineluctable, for practical purposes invisible, as he walked round, trying to peer in.

Ice. If this were the last, it was also the hardest of his tasks, to try to make something of this outrageous glacier. There was no way of dealing with the damned thing, especially with the wand left behind to plug the hole of the eagle eggs. It was utterly silent, impressive, remote, like death. Not for nothing had Dante had the last and most terrible of his infernal circles an icy one; no wonder Oberon thought the princes of this place his ultimate and deadliest Enemy. Barber himself began to experience a sense of depression, of utter futility such as he had seldom experienced. He would a dozen times rather have dealt with

the tricky activity of the kobolds, the treacherous violence of Hirudia, or even endless swarms of double-
headed eagles. There seemed simply nothing he could
do to those glasslike walls.

Wait for day and the sun to melt it? It could not
be long delayed, the moon was paling to its close,
already the stars shone brighter. But, no, that held no
promise of success. The cold dome came down flush
to the ground, with a thin rim of dry grass around it
and beyond that meadow, bespeaking the thought that
this was no ice he knew but some unreasonable variety
that did not melt in the sun.

His teeth were chattering with cold. Perhaps the
only way of penetration was the obvious one. He
stepped up to the smooth surface at random and
swung his sword. It bit deep; great fragments tinkled
and clashed away with every stroke. The ice was soft
or brittle or both. He marked out with his eye space
enough to give him a good tunnel and fell to hewing,
the work warming him.

But as the shards broke out and fell away it became
apparent that the ice was not homogeneous in quality.
A large irregular lump at the heart of the area on
which he was working turned the edge of Barber's
blade while the material around it shattered and cascaded away. This adamantine lump was something
over Barber's own size, and as it took form beneath
the undirected sculpture of his sword it became apparent that it was about his own shape.

With a crash of glasslike crystals, ice avalanched
away from the lump, leaving it standing in the mouth
of the shaft like a snow man in high relief. It was, in
fact, exactly a snow man, or better, an ice man, of
imposing stature, faceless under a domed glassy head-
gear, with a club over its shoulder.

And it began to move; sluggishly with creaking ice
sounds, detaching itself from the remaining matrix,
shifting the club.

Barber stumbled back in alarm, his feet skidding on the unmelted fragments beneath. His sword would not bite, and the wand was far away.

But the creature apparently had no aggressive intentions. After one step it became immobile in its former pose. The starshine shimmered on a film of water, flowing down from some unseen source over the surface and around the ice giant. It froze as it descended and in a moment or two the surface on which Barber had labored was as smooth as ever. The air was cold.

Barber walked fifty paces around the circle of the wall and began chipping again. The ice broke away with the same ease, and as easily as before did an ice giant, complete with club, emerge. Once more the film of water flowed smoothly down and filled the wound. Barber stepped close and touched his hand to the current; it was icy-cold and stung like brine in the wounds the twig had made.

He stepped back, grimacing with pain and shaking off the shining drops. As he did so a couple of them fell on the rose in his buttonhole, the double rose he had plucked at the luchrupán's tree. With a faint sissing sound they dissolved into steam.

Barber stepped back to consider and found that the ends of his now long red beard were covered with tiny particles of rime. Once more he experienced the baffling sense of standing at the edge of discovery, yet somehow lacking the clue that would unlock knowledge. Perhaps the key lay once more in Malacea's injunction to leave his imported habits of thought for those that went with the environment.

But what did that mean in the present case? As a devotee of the mathematically logical approach favored by the newer school of science, he set himself to examine the fundamental assumptions on which he had been working. The first thing that he discovered —somewhat to his own surprise—was that he had been accepting chance as causation. There was something wrong about this; as wrong as his earlier assumption that because the formulas of this existence did not jibe with those he knew, the whole thing was utterly without logic or reason.

Oberon and, still more, Imponens had given him a glimpse of a Fairyland ruled by laws as definite as any he knew, though of a different order. They related more to matters accepted figuratively or not accepted at all in the world he was accustomed to call "his." Probably astrology and numerology would be exact sciences here. Assuredly, he could reject the idea that mere chance had carried him to the encounters with Malacea or the kobolds or the world under the water. The monkeys would write Shakespeare before such a series could come about by accident.

What he had to do was discover the chain of causation and apply it to the present circumstance, shivering outside that dome of ice beneath a cold sky from which the moon had gone, and only faintly tinged with coming day. *The three places.* It had something to do with that; and he was convinced that the third place lay before him, hidden in that impassive hood of ice. Had the others anything in common; was it possible to establish any series?

Apparently not. The first place lay in the heart of the hills and he had reached it by a toilsome journey on foot; the second, under the Pool, and he had attained it by a special adaptation or metamorphosis into a frog. Here was the third, which he hardly could have reached at all without this other special adaptation of wings. . . . Hold on a minute; had not that gauzy-winged fay he met in the skies said something about: "We have in us the light elements, Fire and Air?" Here was series, the series of the Empedoclean elements—Earth for the first place, Water for the second; he had vanquished Air in dealing with those

double-headed eagles. Fire would surely be the anti-
dote to the ice that stood before him.

It was at this point that Fred Barber remembered
how the icy brine had hissed when it touched his rose.
The finding of that flower could be no more chance
than the other events of the series.

Fred Barber plucked the rose from his coat and
advanced to the wall of ice, holding it in front of
him. As far as his fingers could tell it was an ordinary
blossom, but when he came near the ice there was a
hiss and crackle, and water flowed down in a young
torrent, welling out over the grass. A cloud of vapor
rose from it.

The rose melted a deep hemispherical pit in the
face of the ice dome, and of the ice man who had
been there before there was no sign. Barber stepped
into the cavity, holding his new weapon before him.
Beneath his feet was slippery ice and around them
gathered a runnel of coldly steaming water. A step at
a time carried him forward into the tunnel he was
melting, a passage out of dark into dark, with just the
faintest shimmering of rainbow hues where the rising
day behind shot a few beams through. All had a bluish
cast, as though this were the permanent and natural
color of that grim place.

It must have taken half an hour to reach the dark
core of that berg, and an uncontrollable fit of shivering had overtaken him, not entirely due to cold. His
foot felt an edge; he bent, holding the rose downward,
and melted a coating of ice from a granite step, im-
memorially ancient, and rutted deep with the pressure
of many feet. Other steps rose beyond it, leading up to
a monumental double door of bronze. Down them the
melting water cascaded.

When he had cleared the ice from it by using the
rose again, Barber perceived that the door bore a coat
of arms—the same, with crowns and double-headed

eagles that he had now seen twice before. But this time
it was partly overlaid with a more recent plate in plain
brass, into which lettering had been deeply incised.
Barber bent to examine it in the tricky, pulsing light
that came through the ice from the gathering day:

> *"This is the veritable Wartburg. Let him
> enter who has a high heart and the four
> elemental spells; but not unless he can bear
> the eyes of the Redbeard."*

There was something strange about that inscription,
but not until he had already laid hand on the door to
push it open did Barber realize that neither letters
nor words had been English. They were old German,
a language he did not know—or did he? The building
itself had a curious mental atmosphere, as though it
possessed a memory of its own, independent of his,
and were trying to communicate with him, tell him
a great and happy secret. He pushed the door.

It opened slowly, with a musical tinkle of unmelted
ice from the hinges. He was in a hall, high, wide and
deep, blue-dim at the far end, pale blue along the
high windows between the dark uprights. A huge
table ran its whole length, a table in white-streaked
stone that would be marble. At the near end a figure
was seated with its back to Barber, in a chair of horn,
curiously mosaicked together. The figure was wearing
a dark robe and a tall, conical hat, dark blue and
sprinkled with stars.

As Barber came level with him, he perceived this
individual was leaning forward with his elbows on
the table and his chin cupped in his hands. A beard
lay on the table; the face above it was that of Imponens or any other learned doctor in philosophy, with
wide-open eyes staring straight ahead. But he did not
answer when Barber spoke and shook his shoulder,
and the body beneath the robe felt cold.

Barber shuddered slightly and went on down the hall, wondering whether he heard a noise behind him. Toward the far end his eyes focused on figures there. For there were many—a whole row of boys standing against the farther wall, clad in medieval page costumes and with hair to their shoulders, staring stiffly before them like the man in the conical hat. Barber noted that the line had one gap; but what caught and held his eye was the figure in front of the gap.

For this figure also occupied a seat at the table, but the seat was a great carved ivory throne, sweeping up in tall lines to carved double-headed eagles on the pillars at the back. The man himself was leaned forward in an attitude of sleep, his forehead on one arm and chin on the table, and a tall crown of mingled gold and iron, set with jewels, had rolled from his head. All round face and arm lay a great mat of beard, and deeper still, seeming to pass right into the substance of the table itself; and even in that dimness Barber could see that it was red.

A thrill of passionate expectancy, as though he were on the threshold of something at once splendid and terrible, ran through him. He stepped to the table and saw, just beyond the extended fingers, a brass plate let into its top. (Was that a sound again behind him?) Straining his eyes Barber bent close and read:

> *"He shall gain the triple grace*
> *Who reaches this as the third place."*

Clomp.

Barber whirled. Ice men, faceless and menacing, their clubs held aloft, were flooding through the doorway by which he had entered. They deployed into a line across the hall, both sides of the table, and came marching down with ice-creaking steps, ponderous and irresistible.

Barber snatched for the kobold sword, remembered it would not bite on their hardness. The rose? He was surprised to discover it was no longer in his hand; he must have dropped it at the door or when he shook the shoulder of that figure at the other end of the table. For a moment panic jarred through him; then he perceived that the terrible regiment bearing down on him had a gap in its line, the gap caused by the table itself.

He leaped for the table top, and in the very moment of the leap saw a figure at the door behind the ice men; the single page boy missing from the line. The lad's high voice cried: "Time is! The ravens fly no more!" and then Barber's foot touched the brazen plate that was the third place.

It seemed to go right through; he had a sensation of floating disembodied into nothingness. There was a rending crash; the ice without the castle split and shivered away, and a bright new golden sun came streaming in all the windows of that hall, and—

Frederick Barbarossa, he that was Fred Barber, gripped the arms of the ivory throne and stood upright. There was a tug at his chin; the marble table split and its halves toppled to side and side with a booming crash.

"Where is the Enemy?" he demanded, and looked around on ice men that were ice men no longer, but knights and barons in shining mail with swords in hand and a few drops of water shining like jewels on them in the new light.

But that philosopher from the lower end of the table stretched his arms and answered:

"Lord, there is no Enemy, nor ever was, within this place. For the Enemy but shifts from body to body, being impalpable; and being put down in one form, seeks a new and must again be dealt with. This is the end, Lord, for which you were called from sleep, that you might bring the strong power of the iron to the alliance of King Oberon's realm, which is of law. Neither can stand without the other; and now I counsel you that you send straitly to him, since the Enemy in a new guise draws near his borders."

"Let it be done," said Barbarossa.

In the annals of Fairyland the story of that alliance is written—how Barbarossa and his knights journeyed to the west and won a great battle among the sea crags against an invasion of Rakshas, hideous yellow things that lived like ghouls. They were not the last of such invaders, for the Enemy is ubiquitous. But Barbarossa deals hardly with them all; and there is an end of shapings and evil enchantments in that land. These have no power against the iron.

Yet there are whispers and mystery about the great red-bearded King; for it has been observed that when he takes a new love, whether from among the fays or the other people of Fairy, he tells her tales of how he spent some thirty years among the mortals. Some hold that these are merely things that he makes up; for who could believe in a world of such wild unreason that its people must blow each other to bits in order to command obedience to their wills? Some hold, on the other hand, that these tales are nothing but the disturbed dreams that Barbarossa dreamed while lying asleep under the ice, in the Wartburg castle with the ravens circling round. Yet it is observable that there is a certain wild consistency in the King's dreams and his acts; for among his loves he has never taken one from the apple dryads.

END

Dell Bestsellers

- [ ] **THE MEMORY OF EVA RYKER**
  by Donald A. Stanwood $2.50 (15550-9)
- [ ] **BLIZZARD** by George Stone $2.25 (11080-7)
- [ ] **THE BLACK MARBLE**
  by Joseph Wambaugh $2.50 (10647-8)
- [ ] **MY MOTHER/MY SELF** by Nancy Friday $2.50 (15663-7)
- [ ] **SEASON OF PASSION** by Danielle Steel $2.50 (17703-0)
- [ ] **THE IMMIGRANTS** by Howard Fast $2.75 (14175-3)
- [ ] **THE ENDS OF POWER** by H.R. Haldeman
  with Joseph DiMona $2.75 (12239-2)
- [ ] **GOING AFTER CACCIATO** by Tim O'Brien ..$2.25 (12966-4)
- [ ] **SLAPSTICK** by Kurt Vonnegut $2.25 (18009-0)
- [ ] **THE FAR SIDE OF DESTINY**
  by Dore Mullen $2.25 (12645-2)
- [ ] **LOOK AWAY, BEULAH LAND**
  by Lonnie Coleman $2.50 (14642-9)
- [ ] **BED OF STRANGERS**
  by Lee Raintree and Anthony Wilson $2.50 (10892-6)
- [ ] **ASYA** by Allison Baker $2.25 (10696-6)
- [ ] **BEGGARMAN, THIEF** by Irwin Shaw $2.75 (10701-6)
- [ ] **STRANGERS** by Michael de Guzman $2.25 (17952-1)
- [ ] **THE BENEDICT ARNOLD CONNECTION**
  by Joseph DiMona $2.25 (10935-3)
- [ ] **EARTH HAS BEEN FOUND** by D.F. Jones $2.25 (12217-1)
- [ ] **STORMY SURRENDER**
  by Janette Radcliffe $2.25 (16941-0)
- [ ] **THE ODDS** by Eddie Constantine $2.25 (16602-0)
- [ ] **PEARL** by Stirling Silliphant $2.50 (16987-9)

At your local bookstore or use this handy coupon for ordering:

| **Dell** | **DELL BOOKS**
P.O. BOX 1000, PINEBROOK, N.J. 07058 |

Please send me the books I have checked above. I am enclosing $_____
(please add 35¢ per copy to cover postage and handling). Send check or money
order—no cash or C.O.D.'s. Please allow up to 8 weeks for shipment.

Mr/Mrs/Miss_____

Address_____

City_____ State/Zip_____